BRENT MICHAELS

Working Through It All

First published by Brent Michaels 2026

First edition

ISBN: 979-8-9944142-0-0

Editing by Bob Podrasky
Cover art by May Taylor
Proofreading by Amy

This book was professionally typeset on Reedsy.
Find out more at reedsy.com

Alex had never known true love.

On his fiftieth birthday, he remains alone. Throughout his life, he's battled emotional struggles, yearning for a partner who loved him unconditionally — someone who couldn't envision life without him, flaws and all.

Despite this deep desire, he felt unworthy of such love. During his birthday celebration, old destructive patterns resurfaced when he encountered a married man sitting at a nearby table, also celebrating his fiftieth birthday.

Brent Michaels

Contents

I

Author's Note

There's a small part of me in all my characters, but I also include a bit of who I wish I could be.

I love using my imagination, jotting down my thoughts on paper, and crafting stories.

My stories might start dark, but they always end happily ever after.

I sincerely thank you from the bottom of my heart for reading my first book.

I hope you enjoy.

Brent Michaels

1

Chapter One

It was my fiftieth birthday, December 17th, 2005. A significant milestone in my life. Well, to me, anyway. I don't think anyone else cared. My phone wasn't blowing up with the birthday wishes I was hoping for, and the mailman wasn't complaining of a sore back from carrying the hundreds of cards I had hoped to receive. But it felt surreal to me that I was still in existence. It's hard to remember any of the good things that happened during my lifespan, and I know there are many. However, when I take the time to reflect, only the negative aspects of my life come to mind.

We were dining at my favorite Italian restaurant, Marino's, in Toluca Lake—a neighborhood in Los Angeles just around the corner from Warner Bros. Studios—to celebrate my special day. The interior makes you feel as if you've stepped back into the 1950s. Red checkered tablecloths, a candle on each table, along with a bottle of olive oil and vinegar, and a basket of hard, crusty, homemade Italian bread set the scene. I loved the flowered wallpaper that ran throughout the eatery and the artificial grapevines hanging in each arched doorway. And the smells—oh boy, the smells—tomato sauce and garlic filled my senses.

I didn't go there often because it was expensive, but the food was worth every penny. Since my birthday is in December, just a few days before Christmas, I had a hard time finding people to celebrate with me. Most people had Christmas parties to go to and didn't want to miss them.

I've always struggled to make and keep friends, which is another reason I find it hard to find someone to celebrate with me. I'm very insecure and tend to become needy, even with my friends. That's a lot for some people to handle. I constantly need reassurance that I matter to them.

I started asking people to block out the date a month in advance so they wouldn't forget or schedule a Christmas party instead. They always say yes at the time, but when the date approaches, they often claim they forgot and have a Christmas party to attend that night.

For my fiftieth, I asked people I barely liked to celebrate with me. I knew they would be available because they didn't have many close friends themselves. Most people cannot stand them because of their habitual negativity and rudeness. It's not what they say that offends people; it's how they say those words in a sarcastic tone.

I didn't want to spend my fiftieth birthday alone. That would be just sad and very lonely. But it wouldn't be the first special day I've had to celebrate by myself. I understand why I struggle to form and keep friendships. I've tried to change over the years, but I don't seem to be able to make those changes very well on my own.

I know it's unfair to expect others to fix me, but I still hear those old reruns in my head of my parents telling me, "You're stupid, you're lazy, you're just no good." It will take a special person or an exceptional group of friends to tolerate my insecurities.

Five people agreed to go to dinner with me: four men and one woman. None of them were my first choice to celebrate my birthday with me.

"Spending the day with them was better than spending it by myself," I whined out loud to myself.

Jane and I are so much alike that we don't spend a lot of time together. We are both needy people. I only see her after she's broken up with another girlfriend. Lucas and Carl, a very dysfunctional couple, used the excuse that the restaurant was too expensive, so I told them I would pay the entire bill. Then there was Archie. He's the guy who would drop into my life, fuck me hard for a couple of hours, and then I wouldn't see him for a month or two. But this wasn't going to be one of those nights. I was hoping to find a hottie at the dance club we were all going to after dinner.

We were having a pretty fun time talking and laughing. Almost everyone was joking at my expense. People find it easy to make fun of me because of my many insecurities. I hate those jokes, but I laugh at them anyway, so they don't think they bother me. They hurt deeply.

Frank was someone I dated twenty years ago. He told us how his friends would laugh at me. I wasn't like most typical gay men. I didn't want to have sex with all my friends, and to them, this wasn't normal. When I am dating or in a relationship, I am monogamous.

All I've ever wanted was one man to settle down with in a committed relationship—something I have never found in fifty years. I hadn't spoken to Frank in many years, so when I ran into him shopping two weeks ago, out of desperation, I asked if he would like to join us.

While we were eating dinner, the table next to us consisted of three women and three men. The wife of one of the men asked me what we were celebrating.

"It's my fiftieth birthday," I stated cheerfully.

There was no way she and her group couldn't hear how my friends were talking about me.

"It's also my husband's fiftieth birthday today," she said as she pointed at him.

"Congratulations," we said in unison.

He looked up from the table and smiled. For a man celebrating his birthday, he didn't appear pleased. I felt a connection with him as our eyes met—a shared sadness.

"You can't be fifty. My husband looks ten or more years older than you," she added sharply.

He frowned, tilting his head downward toward his plate.

I was in good physical shape at the time, and thanks to family traits, I looked years younger than I was. But I thought it was rude of her to say something like that about her husband in front of their friends and strangers.

She continued to make negative comments about him. He lowered his head like a dog being smacked on its nose with a newspaper.

"Well, I don't have to put up with your vulgar language, lady, so that is one reason I look younger than he does," I said gruffly. This brought a smile to his face. She grimaced.

I thought he was a handsome man. He was about the same

height and weight as me, with brown hair and brown eyes. He had a slight pot belly, which didn't bother me at all. He sat at the end of his table, directly across from me, giving me a full-frontal view. A large bulge in his pants caught my attention. He smiled when he noticed where I was looking. I chuckled and smiled back.

"I'm single," I said sarcastically. "If you don't want him tonight, I'd be happy to take him home with me for my birthday," I added. I smiled at him. He chuckled.

Their friends remained silent throughout the entire exchange. I don't know if these people were closer friends with him or her, but they just sat there with an 'oh my god' expression on their faces.

"He's not that good in bed," she added angrily.

"Lady, I've had enough of this conversation. So thanks for putting a damper on both our birthdays," I replied.

I turned back to my guest and continued eating my chicken parmesan dinner, accompanied by a side of spaghetti and meatballs.

The husband finally grew tired of her and told her to shut up.

"It is my fiftieth birthday. Can you please treat me like a human being for just a few hours?" he barked.

She shot him a dirty look but didn't say anything in return. He sat quietly, eating the remainder of his dinner, and didn't say a word to anyone at his table. The restaurant was crowded as it always is on a Saturday night. The room fell silent as a result of what had transpired. Gradually, voices started to fill the room again. I didn't realize that people around us were paying attention to our banter. Patrons nearby gave the birthday boy one last look of pity.

I paused briefly to think and then turned back toward the

man.

"We're going dancing after dinner. If you would like to join us, you're more than welcome," I said, grinning. He smiled at me but didn't answer.

My dinner guest and I hurried through our meals and desserts so we could leave and do something much happier. We got up from our chairs to leave the restaurant.

"Good night and happy birthday," I said kindly to the man.

We had just walked away from our table when the man said, "Can I still go with you?" I turned to look at him.

His wife, in a thunderous voice, said, "Where the hell do you think you are going?"

"I am going dancing with these nice people," he answered.

Their friends, sitting at their table, looked at him, confused and unsure how to respond.

"Get back to the table," she yelled.

He kept walking away as she continued yelling. He stopped, turned back to her, took the car keys from his pocket, tossed them onto the table, and continued walking away. As she yelled, other patrons in the eatery turned once again to look at her in annoyance. The manager of the establishment immediately walked over to her to find out why she was causing a disturbance.

"We do not allow disturbances like this, ma'am," the manager said firmly. "If you do not start acting civilly, I will ask you and your party to leave." The manager enunciated each word separately and slowly to ensure she understood.

As soon as the birthday boy caught up to me outside the restaurant, he said, "I'm just doing this to make her mad, so don't get any ideas."

"Yes, I know you are," I replied.

He followed the six of us to the parking lot at the side of the restaurant. We all drove our own cars and said we would meet at the bar. The birthday boy was walking a couple of steps behind me, not saying a word. I introduced myself to him while standing on the driver's side of my car with the door open.

"Hi, my name is Alex," I said, smiling.

The birthday boy returned my smile as he stood on the passenger side of the car, his hand on the door handle, ready to open it.

"Hello, my name is Mark," he replied.

"Well, Mark, it is nice to meet you. We are going to a gay bar to dance. Are you okay with that?" I asked.

Mark hesitated for a moment before answering.

"Yes, we have a few gay friends, or my wife has a few gay friends whom we've gone dancing with before," he replied, stumbling over his words.

He paused another moment before he continued speaking.

"But it has been a while, and I was a little skinnier back then," he said uncomfortably.

I smiled at him and said caringly, "You look simply fine to me."

He smiled as he turned his head away. We drove to Oil Can Harry's in Studio City, not far from the restaurant. He's a lot cuter when he smiles, I thought.

"I'm a little nervous to be dancing in front of others," Mark said.

"Don't worry, I'll protect you," I replied. Mark chuckled.

"Well, I'm not a good dancer either, if that's what you're worried about. I like to bounce around and have fun, acting silly," I said.

Many people have told me I am a good dancer. I am not a

trained dancer. Nearly twenty years ago, I tried my hand at acting. I sang, danced, and acted in several plays around Los Angeles. That career never took off, but it was fun trying. I met a lot of wonderful people who were working towards the same goal. Sadly, I did meet a lot of not-so-nice people, usually ugly, fat men who had some pull in the industry and said they could get me a part in a movie or TV show if I would have dinner with them, aka, fuck me. I always said no. Why was it never a hot guy who asked me that question?

I told Mark I wasn't a good dancer because I didn't want him to be self-conscious about being a little out of shape. He looked good to me.

I like to take my shirt off while dancing to see how much attention I can get. And tonight I wanted to get some attention from a handsome man, hopefully a handsome man with a large penis.

Outside the bar in the back parking lot, I ran into Jeff, the guy I buy my weed from. He delivers it to my condo once a month. I buy the good, expensive stuff, and he likes to hook up with me if I'm not dating anyone. He asked if I wanted a hit off his joint.

"Absolutely. You know I love your pot," I said with a large smile.

I hoped it would be the strong stuff he delivers to my home. I took one long hit because I wanted it to last a while. I was going to ask Jeff if Mark could have a hit when Mark asked, "Can I have a hit?"

"Sure, if you are on a date with Alex tonight," Jeff replied.

Mark leaned toward me, kissed my cheek, and said, "Yes, I am."

I was caught off guard by Mark's kiss. He smiled and took a long hit just like I did. As we left the parking lot, Jeff stayed near the back of the building, talking with friends. Mark and I walked to the club's front entrance, where we rejoined my dinner guests. Several people booed, thinking we were cutting, until I explained we were all together for my birthday.

While waiting in line, Mark said, "Don't get any ideas because I kissed your cheek. I just wanted some pot."

I placed my hand on Mark's shoulder and said, "No problem. I respect your boundaries, and I know you're straight. So no touching. But if you change your mind," I said. Mark chuckled.

"I need an escape from my wife, and pot gives me the release I need."

"I use pot for the same reason. I stress out over the tiniest things, and it drives me crazy until I figure it out," I said. "I have to tell you something." Mark gave me a curious look. "I get a little clingy when I am stoned in public, so don't think I am coming on to you."

Mark chuckled and said it wouldn't bother him.

As we entered the club, the music transitioned from a soft muffle to a thunderous thump, thump, thump. It took us a while to get inside because the line ran from the front door to the rear of the building. Just inside the door, the club manager collected the cover charge from everyone who entered. He was a heavy smoker, and the tip of his mustache that touched his upper lip had turned orange. I could smell the stale tobacco odor on his breath as he spoke.

"Who's the handsome stud standing behind you?" the manager asked.

Mark's cheeks turned red as he grinned.

"He's straight, so don't get any ideas," I told the manager as I paid him the cover fee for both of us.

"Dang, he's hot," the manager said as he looked Mark over

from head to toe.

"Even if he wasn't, I don't think it would work out between you," I said, giggling.

"Why?" the manager asked.

"I think he's definitely a top, and so are you, so you've told me many times," I replied.

The manager laughed. Mark cleared his throat. I chuckled.

Mark bought the first round of drinks and said, "Happy Birthday," as we clinked glasses.

"I'll get the next round," I said. "And a Happy Birthday to you, too." We clinked our glasses together once more.

There were three bars inside the club: two downstairs and one upstairs in the lounge, where you could have a quiet talk with someone. My favorite bartender, Dan, was always working at the front bar near the dance floor. He was extremely popular with all ages. He was handsome, kind of like Tab Hunter, a heartthrob from the sixties. He was around thirty-five years old, with blond hair and blue eyes, standing close to six feet tall. His well-toned body was accentuated by a prominent bulge in his tight white jeans and blue tank top. I'd been asking him for two years, since he started working at this club, if his bulge in his pants was real or just a pair of socks to attract customers. He'd give me a broad smile and tell me to have fun with the young boys who chased me around the dance floor. His words alone made my night. He knew me well enough to know the younger men were always after me.

I have an above-average face that many find pleasing, so I've been told. I worked hard to maintain my well-toned body and my washboard stomach. And being the age I am, the younger men love me. However, I'm still partial to men between forty and fifty years old, just as I was in my twenties.

My friends from dinner were already on the other side of the club near the back bar. I think from the moment we all entered, they had already forgotten about me, even though I paid for everyone's dinner. I don't remember them thanking me for dinner or even wishing me a happy birthday. They made no effort to find me. There was more space to stand and talk to friends at the back bar. People who loved to dance gathered at the front of the club, and socializers stayed at the back.

The pot we smoked outside wasn't very strong, which was disappointing, because my buzz was already wearing off. I left Mark standing at the edge of the dance floor and told him I'd be right back. I knew the DJ—Peter—who was playing eighties disco tunes and wanted to say hello. Peter was twenty-eight and on the heavier side. I only knew him from the club and didn't know what his day job was, but he spun the best disco around. He was always laughing and ready with a smile.

"Could you send my friend Mark a fiftieth birthday wish between songs?" I asked.

"No problem," he replied.

Mark stood anxiously at the edge of the dance floor, waiting for me to return. Many of the younger men who had spotted Mark were moving in for the kill. Mark kept an eye on me to make sure I was coming back. I returned as quickly as possible. I didn't want him to get overwhelmed by the twenty-somethings who were attempting to talk to him. I could see the tension in his body relax as I approached him.

"Don't worry. I won't desert you for a hotter man," I told him. He chuckled.

Without realizing it, I had given up my search for a man with a large penis and decided to ensure that Mark had a good birthday. I grabbed his hand and pulled him onto the dance floor, where some of my younger friends were already dancing. I called everyone my friend, even if it wasn't true. That way, I didn't feel so pathetic. He looked surprised, but not for the reason I expected. When I let go of his hands, he quickly placed them in front of him.

"You okay?" I asked.

He didn't say anything. He motioned with his eyes for me to look down. As I did, he lifted his hands so I could see what was wrong. He had an erection, which was very obvious through the silky fabric of the dress pants he was wearing. He put his hands back in front of him, leaned over to get near my ear, and uttered, "Pot makes me horny, and I wear boxers." We both laughed. He didn't appear upset and seemed comfortable pointing it out to me.

The club was dark except for the disco lights flashing and twirling. The dance floor was packed with men swaying against each other, so it was easy for Mark to hide his boner. I wanted his boner to mean more than it did. Did I turn him on? Were the twenty-somethings turning him on? I believed him about the pot. The strong pot I smoke at home does the same thing to me. But the pot we smoked earlier did nothing.

"Let's start dancing so we can get you distracted, because if the younger guys see that bulge in your pants, they will be on you like flies to honey," I stated with a big smile.

I enjoyed dancing with the group already on the dance floor because they always paid a lot of attention to me. I'm not usually into guys in their early twenties, but when I needed attention and no one my age was available, they were always willing and able to give me what I needed. Not every young guy is a bottom, but I am, so I need a top. There's always a young guy who brags about his big dick and likes to top an older man.

My favorite young man, whom I've taken home a few times, calls his big dick his show-stopper. I'm not sure about that, but it definitely makes my eyes roll back in my head. I love his red hair, from the top of his head to the tips of his toes. All it ever cost me was a good breakfast at the corner diner near my condo the next morning.

No one in the bar knew it was my birthday, except for my dinner companions, so no special wishes were coming my way. It felt a little childish to tell everyone it was my birthday. I did mention it when we joined my dinner friends in line, so the people who booed didn't kill us, but even they didn't say happy birthday to me. I had hoped maybe Mark would have mentioned it to someone on the dance floor, but he didn't know any of the people dancing around us, so who would he tell?

While the DJ was between songs, he sent a fiftieth birthday wish to Mark as I pointed down to where he was on the dance floor. Mark, a little embarrassed, turned bright red. The crowd cheered. As soon as the DJ announced Mark's birthday, more young men swarmed around him. Fifty-year-old men are like catnip to the younger crowd when someone is looking for a sugar daddy.

I believe Mark enjoyed the attention even though he pretended otherwise. It made me happy to see a smile cross his face after his evening had started off so badly. I felt a few flashes of jealousy over the attention Mark was getting. Usually, the young men paying attention to Mark were the ones chasing me. However, Mark was the new meat in the bar that night. But every time I saw a smile on his handsome face, those feelings quickly faded.

Mark seemed to be enjoying himself as he danced with the young men around us, or maybe he was just stoned. As I started to sweat, I took off my dress shirt, then my T-shirt, like a striptease. I think I surprised Mark with how fit I was as he stared at my washboard stomach while a couple of the younger men nearby ran their hands over me, and the others hooted and howled.

When the music was good, my body was all over the place. One night, while dancing, I received a note from a young lady that read, "You can tell how a man is in bed by the way he dances, and you must be heaven." I thought about going home with her that night, but it had been ten years since I had last been with a woman, so I decided not to because I didn't want to upset the balance of the universe. However, I also didn't want to disappoint her after the wonderful note she had given me.

I've often disappointed men in the bedroom over the years. I have a rugged exterior, and many have asked, "Are you a fireman?" They think I should have a large penis and enjoy being on top. But when we get into bed, they find out that I have an average-sized dick and I love being on bottom, getting ravaged by a prominent appendage. So, over the years, I make sure my suitor knows I am a bottom.

I enjoy dancing with someone who moves like me, and Mark was doing a good job of it. I believe Mark's boner problem had disappeared because I no longer saw any sign of it tenting his pants. But I was still fantasizing about its size because of the tent it made. He told me earlier, before we started dancing, that he used to love working out and being more active to stay in shape. But over time, he just stopped caring about himself because of how verbally abusive his wife was. While we were dancing, I imagined him with his shirt off, his well-toned body on display, and our sweaty chests rubbing against each other. Then I came back to reality.

He leaned in close to my ear while dancing and said, "I love being stoned. It's my escape from reality."

Mark didn't remember telling me earlier, which I thought was cute. But I guess the pot was strong enough for him. He was grinning from ear to ear and bouncing around on the dance floor with everyone else. I wondered how long it had been since he smiled this much in one night.

One of the young men dancing with us asked Mark if he would go home with him. Mark's eyes widened in surprise. After a pause, Mark smiled and said, "I thank you for the invite, but I am on a date with Alex tonight."

"Well, Alex is a lucky man. I hope I see you again sometime," said the young man.

Mark had a shocked look on his face. He leaned into my ear and whispered what the young man had said. I smiled at him.

"See, you are hot. Your wife is crazy," I replied. Mark smiled.

After a couple of hours on the dance floor, we were both exhausted and very sweaty.

"I'm ready to go home," I told Mark.

"To your house?" he replied nervously.

"Well, where do you live?" I asked.

"Brentwood," he replied.

"That's forty-five minutes away. I'm too tired for a ninety-minute round trip," I said.

I paused for a moment.

"I can drop you off at a nearby hotel," I said dismissively, "or you can come home with me?"

He grimaced.

"I'm still mad at my wife, and I don't want to go home yet... So, can I come home with you?" he mumbled.

We were standing near the front bar when I looked down at

the front of Mark's pants. His hands were in his front pockets, and his boner was back.

As Mark and I left through the front entrance, I paused and looked back at the front bar. Dan, the bartender, was looking at me, surprised. This was the first time in two years I forgot to say goodbye and leave him a big tip. I asked Mark to wait for me.

"I'll be right back," I told Mark.

I hurried back to Dan. I took two twenties out of my pocket and handed them to him.

"Sorry, Dan. It's been a tough day," I said kindly. He smiled.

As Mark stood on the passenger side of my car, and I was on the driver's side in the club's parking lot, he said, "But remember..."

"Yes, I know, nothing is going to happen," I said, in a frustrated tone.

I was beginning to doubt him more and more.

2

Chapter Two

My condo was just a few minutes from the bar, in a small neighborhood of mostly condo buildings. I was still a little high when we arrived. My buzz was fading, which was kind of boring, and I was ready for another good hit. I hadn't asked Mark if he still felt high, but as soon as we entered my condo, Mark asked, "Do you have any pot in the house?"

"Yep, sure do," I replied quickly, "I always have pot in the house."

I used pot almost every night to help me relax after a stressful day at work. Sometimes, it's the only way I can fall asleep. Managing a post-production video company filled with prima donnas is stressful. Everyone thinks they are special, both clients and employees. Plus, I have a boss who threatens my job when a client complains about something trivial, so that they can get a discount on the final bill.

"Can we do another hit?" Mark asked.

"My pot is much stronger than what we had earlier," I said, grinning.

"Excellent," he proclaimed.

After taking a good hit, he sat on the sofa, smiled widely, and said, "WOW, this is good pot. The only bad thing about pot this strong is that it makes me so horny that I could fuck almost anything. I am so hard right now."

I smiled and let out a soft moan as I saw his boner through his silky pants. His dick looked much bigger at my condo than it did at the poorly lit bar.

"Do you have any porn?" he asked.

I grinned.

This Mark isn't as shy as the man I met at the restaurant a few hours ago, when he's stoned—let's say super stoned. He wasn't this bold at the bar either. I didn't know what might happen, if anything, or if he's as horny as he claimed. I exhaled a deep breath as many dirty thoughts swirled in my mind.

I showed him where the porn was in the bottom drawer of the TV stand. I turned on the DVD player and the TV, then handed him the remotes. I had an extensive collection of both gay and straight porn. I preferred straight porn over gay porn because I thought the men in straight porn were better looking and more effective at completing their tasks.

I took a deep hit of pot, then hurried to the bathroom connected to my bedroom to freshen up. I told Mark he could use the bathroom halfway down the hall if he needed to. While in my bathroom, I heard the toilet in the hallway bathroom flush. Just in case I could persuade Mark to do something with me, I made sure I was prepared for him. Not knowing if he had ever had sex with a man, I didn't want any surprises that might upset him.

By the time I finished freshening up, my pot had fully kicked in. I felt braver when stoned and less afraid to ask for what I wanted. I changed into my gym shorts and a T-shirt before heading back to the living room. They were easier to remove when necessary. I loved my stronger pot. It was as if I were floating, and my body was tingling. I was horny, and my butt was on high alert. The pot had the same effect on me as it did on Mark. I was hard, and I wanted to get fucked and fucked hard.

As I came around the corner into the living room from the hallway, Mark was watching porn, naked, not even a pair of socks, on my sofa, jerking off. My eyes opened wide. I gasped for a breath of air. He looked up at me without stopping what he was doing and didn't seem to be embarrassed one little bit.

"I hope you don't mind, but I am just so horny right now and so stoned. This is really good pot," he exclaimed, with his legs stretched out in front of him. "I could go into the bathroom to finish myself off if this bothers you, but I need the visual effect of porn to reach climax."

"Continue ... Please ... It's your birthday," I said, motioning with my hands as if I were conducting an orchestra.

I was barely able to catch my breath as I watched him stroke his uncut, long, thick shaft from base to tip. It had to be at least ten inches long, and fat, so fat. I took a deep breath, then exhaled so hard I saw the curtains move slightly a few feet away.

When I saw his boner through his pants just moments ago, I was amazed at how big it looked. But with no pants on and out in the open, it was so much bigger and more beautiful. He was one hairy guy from head to toe. I thought his little pot belly was so cute as it wiggled while he pulled on his dick. He stroked his shaft from top to bottom. Small moans escaped his lungs. He moved one hand gently up and down his shaft while the other hand held his balls. My breathing became more difficult as I watched him.

As his hand reached the top of his penis, he pulled all the foreskin up to completely cover the head. As all my breath left my lungs, a whisper came out of me. "Oh my god." I could feel my mouth watering, and I swallowed.

Once I learned how to breathe again, I asked, "Can I join you on the sofa?"

"Sure. It's your house," he replied.

I quickly undressed and sat beside him. I wanted to touch his dick, but I didn't. I didn't want to scare him. I didn't know the rules of this game yet. I started to jerk off as soon as I sat down.

"This is the strongest pot I have ever smoked," Mark uttered.

I had a big smile on my face as I watched him stroke his enormous dick. I felt very inadequate sitting next to such a large appendage.

"Have you ever jerked off with another guy before?" I asked cautiously.

He smiled and said, "Not since I was fourteen with my best friend."

That must mean he's never been with a man before, I thought.

In the porn video Mark was watching, the lady had just started sucking the man's dick. Mark inhaled a deep breath and released a soft moan. With much intensity, he pulled harder at the head of his dick.

"My god, would that feel good right now to have my dick sucked?" Mark mumbled.

I perked up immediately.

"I'd be happy to help you out," I said enthusiastically.

With no hesitation, he replied, "If I weren't so stoned, I

wouldn't, but would you please suck my dick?"

I didn't say a word; I just went down on him.

His dick was so large that I could barely fit my mouth around it. Somehow, I made it work. Nothing was going to stop me. I didn't want to disappoint him or myself. It felt so good in my mouth. It had been several weeks since I'd last had sex with anyone. And it had been forever since I'd had a dick of this size. I sucked hard. I went down on it as far as I could. I sucked the head, and I licked the shaft. I love uncut dicks. What a great birthday for me. From the sounds coming from him, I must have been doing a good job. The more he moaned, the harder I sucked.

Mark gave me instructions on how to suck his dick. I didn't mind at all. I was happy as long as it was in my mouth. I wished he'd had a shower before I went down on him. I took a quick bird bath before returning to the living room, but he had not. He was a little smelly from the sweat from dancing. He tasted very salty. I didn't want to suggest a shower before we continued because I was afraid that everything would come to a screeching halt, and I didn't want to miss out on this beautiful dick on my special day.

He slid down on the sofa so he could spread his legs wider like the guy in the video, and he told me to lick his balls. He quickly changed from asking me to ordering me to do what he wanted. His voice changed from soft to husky in one breath. Salty or not, I was not going to let that stop me. I had to fight my way through all of the hair covering his ball sack. For someone who'd said he didn't want a man to touch him, I was touching a lot. While licking his balls, he continued jerking off. His testicles were enormous, and his sack was plenty large enough to hold them. I buried my face into them. I had to keep remembering to breathe.

"I'm getting close. Suck my dick," he exclaimed.

When I started sucking, he told me to jerk him off at the same time. I followed his instructions with gusto. I didn't want to miss out on this one-time opportunity with him. It's not often that I find a beautiful piece of meat like this to play with. As I continued sucking and jerking him off, his speech became mumbled. "I'm... I'm going... I'm going to..."

The loudest groan came out of him just as his large load escaped his penis, hitting hard at the back of my throat. I gagged a little, but I kept my lips wrapped tightly around the head as he filled my mouth. My lips remained tightly around his dick while I waited till he had spilled his last drop. He was lifeless. I was about ready to swallow when he ordered, "Swallow" breathlessly—just one word. I followed my order and swallowed. I drank up every drop. He tasted so good.

I looked at him with a big smile on my face as his dick popped out of my mouth, and then I said, "Happy birthday to us." He nodded his head to acknowledge.

We rested for a moment. Mark sprawled out on the sofa, lifeless, with my head lying on his lap. We needed to catch our breath.

"Got more pot?" Mark asked.

I perked up quickly.

"Yep," I said happily, thinking, we're not finished yet.

Mark was functioning better than I was. I usually take only one hit of my strong pot per night. Otherwise, I'm toast and can barely walk from the sofa to my bed, and then the next morning, I feel a little hungover. Even though he had just had an orgasm, he was still hard. Usually, guys with big dicks go soft immediately after an orgasm, which is always bad when I haven't reached mine yet. They're done for the night, so I have to finish myself off. I couldn't believe that this long, thick dick with large balls and a low-hanging sack was sitting on my sofa for my birthday and was still hard. It was a beautiful sight. Plus, it's more fun smoking pot with someone on your birthday.

Mark got up from the sofa and put in another video. I chuckled as he walked across the room to the TV. His hard dick swung from side to side like a metronome, one of those music timers musicians use.

"I put in a gay one for you," he said.

"Thanks," I replied.

"What part of the video do you like?" he asked.

"I... I like the fucking," I said hesitantly, but hoping I could push him in that direction.

He kept clicking the fast-forward button on the remote until he got to the fucking. The men were doing it doggy style. He seemed to be enjoying the gay porn, I thought, because of the grin on his face. I didn't say anything to him about it.

He started playing with his dick again while we watched the two men fuck.

"I love getting fucked when I am stoned," I stated softly.

After a brief pause, he said, "I'll fuck you."

"Would you?" I said excitedly. "You can fuck me as hard as you want to, and in any position. I just need to get fucked."

I loved someone with a large dick taking control of my ass. And being super stoned, I knew that I could take whatever he dished out. There was no kissing or foreplay, except for that great blow job. He gave me no sign that he wanted to kiss. I grabbed the lube from the cabinet under the coffee table, which I kept there for emergencies like this. I knew the condoms I had would not fit his enormous dick, so I said nothing. He told me he had never been with a man before, so I knew we were safe, because I always am. Plus, I just had my last HIV test two weeks ago, which was negative.

He bent me over the sofa, my knees on the floor, as I lay face down on the cushions. I handed him the lube, and he knew just what to do. He put some lube in his right hand and lubed up his penis and my butt. There was no romance in his actions, just a sexual act. He took his dick in his right hand and aligned it to my butthole. He pushed straight inside me with no hesitation. With the head of his penis inside me, it opened me up, and "Oh my god" came out of my mouth. He pushed himself the rest of the way in until his body was tight against mine.

I loved the feeling of his warm body tight against my backside and how he filled me up. I have always loved getting fucked, but when I was stoned the way I was that night, every nerve ending in my body was on high alert, and I enjoyed it even more. I was glad that I hadn't had an orgasm yet. Sometimes I cannot get fucked if I've already had an orgasm. It can be painful. I gasped for air because it had been a long time since anything that large had been inside me. He pulled it almost all the way out until just the head remained inside me, and he asked in a controlling voice, "You said I can do whatever I want to do to you, correct?"

"Yes, you can," I replied.

But what he did caught me off guard. He fucked me hard. Fucked me like a man just released from prison. He shoved his dick inside me in one fast, inward motion. Every ounce of air I had in my lungs was pushed out. He kept railing me like a jackhammer destroying a ten-inch slab of concrete until it was demolished. All the way in, and all the way out, and back in again. Hard and fast. I was having trouble breathing as I kept rambling, "Oh my, oh my, oh my god." He chuckled in an evil tone and slammed against me even harder.

He didn't stop pushing forward until his body was tight against mine. I could feel his balls slap against me. His length and thickness hurt and felt great at the same time as he plunged himself deep inside me. No one had ever fucked me like this before. Not even the older men with large dicks who liked to fuck me hard when I was in my twenties. They would use me and throw me away like a used napkin. I was always devastated.

As he continued to fuck me, I could barely catch my breath. My body was in ecstasy with every nerve ending energized. My heart was beating faster than I thought it ever could. He hammered me in that position for several minutes without stopping as the moans kept escaping from my lungs. He pulled himself out of me and ordered me in a commanding voice to lie on my back. I felt empty without him inside me. I flipped onto my back quickly. He grabbed my feet and threw my legs over my head. As soon as my legs were in the air, he entered me and returned to pulverizing my ass once again.

I enjoyed every minute of it. His fat dick was massaging my hole for my birthday. This was what I needed. I was lonely. He made me feel wanted. But because of the size, I was once again glad I was stoned. I was not afraid of his commanding voice, the way I was with the men who controlled me when I was younger. I obeyed every order he barked out. His voice deepened with every command he uttered.

"Don't touch yourself while I fuck you!" he ordered. "Put your hands over your head and don't put them down until I say you can."

I wanted to touch myself so badly because my hole was hurting, but I did not. I believe he was taking his anger for his wife out on my ass. He kept pounding me harder and harder as his breathing became deeper and deeper. The look on his face grew increasingly intense. He was going to make me come without touching myself.

"I'm going to... I'm going... I'm going to..." I tried to say, knowing I was close to an orgasm.

"If you come, I'm not going to stop fucking you until I'm done. So it's up to you whether you come or not," he uttered.

His words had so much desperation in them. I needed and wanted this to happen, regardless of his reasons. My insecurities made me do many strange things, even if it meant letting someone abuse me. I had no choice. I wasn't touching myself. He kept fucking me hard until I came. My balls pulled up tight against me, and my release shot over my head. He wasn't kidding; he kept fucking me.

My butthole was on fire. I didn't want to break my word to him. Was he lying about never being with a man, or was he simply in denial about his true nature? I don't think it was a lie. I didn't want it to be a lie. I have seen pot make guys so horny that they just whip out their dicks, jerk off, shoot, put it back in their pants, and go back to whatever they were doing before. If I had been home tonight by myself and smoked pot, I would have had my big dildo up my ass.

Mark told me to grab my ankles so he didn't have to hold them up any longer. I followed his orders. He put his hands directly on the floor and arched his body over mine. He continued ramming my butt as hard as he could, coming straight down on me until his body was tightly against mine. With every slam against me, I could feel the air in my lungs leave my body. My butt was feeling like it was going to explode. Almost five minutes had gone by since I came. No one has ever fucked me that long after I reached an orgasm. I kept watching what he was doing to my butt in amazement. I could feel the burning and the pain as he moved inside me. I loved watching his large penis go in and out of me. I loved watching his hairy body hover over me. I was so stoned that I fantasized he was a grizzly bear attacking me.

"I'm going to come," he growled.

His words were barely coherent enough for me to understand. As he came, he rammed himself inside me as hard as he could, pushing against my prostate with all his energy. I think my eyes rolled back into my head, and I almost passed out.

After his last slam against me, he collapsed on top of me, breathing heavily and still inside me. I couldn't believe that he was still hard. I could feel his penis pulsating inside me as if it had its own heartbeat. Usually, after we were done, I would place light kisses on the face and neck of the person who had fucked me, but Mark still never gave me any sign that he wanted to kiss.

While lying on top of me and still inside me, I squeezed my butt muscles around his softening penis. This made him moan every time I squeezed. My butt was so sore that it felt like his penis was still growing inside me. We were sweaty, sticky, sloppy, and luckily not messy after a fucking like that. For all the noise he was making and all the instructions he was giving me, he was now almost silent except for his deep, steady breaths. I wanted to go to sleep. I was exhausted. My butt was still on fire. I had only one bed, so he had to sleep with me.

"We need to shower before going to bed," I uttered.

As he removed his penis from my butt, my body jerked from the sensitivity of my hole.

"Oh my," I said.

I could feel my butt relax as it left my body. I felt so empty without him inside me. I guided him into the shower. He washed himself from head to toe, and I told him to go to bed. He didn't protest when I explained that I had just one bed. I finished cleaning myself, then got into bed opposite him. I had a California king-size bed, so there was plenty of room for both of us to sleep comfortably.

Mark was as far on his side of the bed as he could get. He lay there quietly.

"I need to do one more thing before going to sleep," I told him softly.

I leaned in and kissed the back of his neck. He didn't move.

"Thank you for my birthday present," I added. He didn't reply, so maybe he had already fallen asleep.

I could barely keep my eyes open. I was exhausted, and my butt was tender. The clock on the nightstand read 4:00 a.m. I thought about my day and couldn't make sense of any of it. I was now fifty years old. Where did all the time go? I had hoped my dinner companions would have told the entire club that it was my birthday. I wanted someone to make a fuss over me. But I was content having this hairy man in my bed. How did I end up getting involved with a married man? I rolled onto my side, hugging a pillow, and fell asleep.

3

Chapter Three

I woke up around noon on Sunday when I heard the church bells ringing from the Catholic church at the end of my street. If it weren't for those damn bells chiming, I probably would have slept a bit longer. My eyes slowly opened, feeling like they were glued shut. The first thing I thought about was that my ass hurt. I still felt a little stoned because I usually don't smoke that much pot at once.

Mark woke up a few minutes after I did in a panic because he had not communicated with his wife since late yesterday evening. He panicked again when he saw me lying in bed next to him. Pot doesn't make you lose your memory, but for a moment, he pretended that it did.

"Oh my god. What did I do?" he shouted.

"You fucked me hard, that's what you did," I said, chuckling.

"I know my wife can be a bitch, but I've never cheated on her before, especially with a man. If it weren't for the pot, I wouldn't have done that with you. I don't know you. What if I bring a disease home to my wife?" he exclaimed.

"Well, if you're telling me the truth about never cheating and that you have never been with a man before ... I know we're safe, because I have only had safe sex with others until last night, and all my HIV tests are always negative," I told him.

That's why I didn't suggest condoms last night. Plus, I don't think I have a condom that would fit that thing anyway." He gave me a stern look. "And you could have mentioned condoms at any time if they were so important to you," I exclaimed. "But for some reason, I trusted you. I can't tell you why I trusted you, because normally I don't trust anyone. But I felt safe with you, for some reason," I added.

We both fell quiet for a few seconds.

"I have to tell you, you're very good at sex," I muttered.

"My wife doesn't think so," he replied.

"Well, maybe with all her complaining, you just lost interest in her. Or maybe you have been looking for someone like me to play with for a while now, just maybe?" I remarked.

Mark didn't respond to my comment, but he did try to hide the slight grin that came to the corner of his mouth.

"How long has it been since you had sex with your wife?" I asked.

Mark had to think for a minute before answering.

"More than a year, I believe."

"No wonder you unloaded so much sperm last night." I grinned.

"It's not like I don't jerk off all the time. I still have a strong sex drive but wish I didn't," he replied.

"Do you watch porn at home?" I asked curiously.

"Some."

"Do you watch gay porn?" I asked.

Mark hesitated, then said.

"Yes, I do."

"No wonder you knew what to do last night." I chuckled.

I told Mark that if he was so worried about his wife, he should call her.

"Tell her that you were so angry that you stayed at a hotel overnight and will take a taxi home later today."

Mark went into the living room to call his wife. I heard him say excitedly, "Oh my god."

I walked quickly to the living room to see what was wrong. Mark pointed to the sofa and the carpet where he railed me last night. But I looked at the naked man standing in my living room with the big dick instead. It took my breath away. I had to chuckle when I saw his hairy body in the daylight. I didn't think I'd ever seen anyone that hairy.

Even though my ass was sore, and I do mean sore, I wanted him to fuck me again.

"Look at the sofa," Mark said loudly, pointing at the sofa.

I laughed when I looked. Lube was covering the couch and carpet where I got screwed. Boy, did I get screwed.

"Well, it's not the first time I've had to clean up a mess after getting laid," I told him. "That's what the mini carpet cleaner is for." I giggled. Mark chuckled. I like seeing him laugh, I thought.

Before Mark called his wife, I told him that I would be taking a shower, and he should join me afterward. He calmed down some after talking to his wife, but he did hang up on her because all she did was yell at him. Mark never bothered to put clothes on as he roamed around my condo. He seemed to be so relaxed as he walked around naked. I enjoyed watching his big dick and low-hanging sack flop around as he walked.

With every step I took, my butt reminded me of what Mark did to me last night. I couldn't get rid of the large grin on my face. After his call, he came into the shower. I had a large shower with a shower head on each side. He stayed on the opposite end so as not to touch me. I watched him as he washed every part of his body. I was getting aroused as he washed his dick. He turned towards me. I was standing across from him with an erection.

"No, not again, never," Mark stated as he stared at my boner.

"I so enjoyed last night, Mark. You gave me a fantastic birthday present. If you ever decide to do it again, I'm more than willing," I said caringly.

"No, I can't," he exclaimed.

"But you want to, don't you?" I responded.

"No, I can't," he replied.

"That wasn't the question, was it?" I asked.

He sighed, surrendering, because he knew that he wanted to. I smiled at him and got out of the shower. The shower doors were clear glass. As I dried off, I kept watching Mark as he rinsed off. He watched me from the corner of his eye, pretending like he wasn't looking at me. I didn't pretend anything; I was looking straight at him. He turned his head.

My conversation with him in the shower must have had an effect because his dick was getting hard. I couldn't help but smile. Just looking at it made me take a deep breath. I wondered how much blood it took to fill that thing, and did he get lightheaded when he had an erection? He looked at me to see if I was paying attention to him. I smiled and walked into the bedroom.

I was almost fully dressed when Mark entered my bedroom

from the bathroom naked. I thought that he wanted me to see his half-erect penis; otherwise, he could have wrapped his towel around himself. I felt so sorry for the confusion he was living in. I know he wanted to say yes to everything, but he was at war with himself. I knew he wanted to say yes because he never put on any clothes; he wanted me to look at him.

"Don't read anything into my erection," he commented. He paused to catch his breath.

"For a fifty-year-old man, I still have a strong sex drive, so I still get erections without much effort," he stated.

He had a scared look on his face as he sat on the edge of the bed, starting to put on the same socks he wore last night. I tossed him a clean pair of my socks and underwear and told him to put them on. I knew he was going to object, but I spoke first.

"Tell your wife you bought them at the hotel so you didn't have to wear home the dirty ones," I said firmly.

Mark sat quietly on the bed, saying nothing.

"I respect your wishes, and nothing will happen again if that's what you truly want," I added.

Mark put on the underwear and socks.

"Thanks again for last night. I had a wonderful birthday because of you. Plus, I had not enjoyed someone's penis like that in a very long time," I uttered kindly.

As I thanked him, his penis started to go up again. He looked at me with fear on his face. He was more excited than he wanted to be. I smiled at him mischievously as his dick popped through the slit in the boxers. I leaned down to kiss him on the lips, but he pushed me away, doing so gently, not with anger. But he didn't move any farther away from me either.

I put my hand on his upper chest and pushed him slowly onto

his back so he could lie comfortably on the bed. His penis was hard and pointing upward through the boxers. He looked so cute, but scared. Even though my jaws were still sore from sucking him last night, I put him back into my mouth.

"I shouldn't," he uttered.

He put his right hand against my chest to stop me. But as my mouth closed around his dick, his hands relaxed, falling onto the bed, and he surrendered to me.

While I sucked his penis, mainly at the head, he began stroking himself at the base with the three-finger method. It's like milking a cow. It didn't take him long to come. I wrapped my lips around him as I did last night, pulling my lips off tightly so I didn't lose a drop. He tasted great. I looked at him and smiled.

"Thank you for another birthday present," I said.

I reached for his hand, pulling him into an upright sitting position. He looked at me and grinned.

"Time to get dressed and get something to eat at the diner down the street. Then I will drive you home," I told him.

As we ate a late breakfast, we talked about what we enjoy doing in our free time. Mark said he doesn't do things like he used to because he doesn't have many close friends anymore. His wife had run them all off.

Mark's likes and dislikes are similar to mine, including baseball, beach volleyball, drag racing, basketball, camping, fishing, hiking, and exercising. Mark no longer hikes or exercises much because he lost interest in them. He had stopped taking care of himself.

"You need to start taking care of yourself again," I said, caringly. He just shrugged at me.

"I mean it, Mark. You're a nice guy, and you know how to

fuck." Mark laughed.

"That's better. You need to laugh more. So please take care of yourself."

I dropped Mark off a couple of blocks from his house, where he told me. I gave him one of my business cards with my private phone number on it, but I never thought he would call.

"I don't want it," he stated firmly. So I stuck it into his shirt pocket anyway, just in case he changed his mind.

Mondays are one of my busiest days at work. Editing, audio, and graphic sessions take place throughout the weekend. I need to catch up on paperwork, call the clients to ensure they are satisfied with their weekend sessions, and follow up with the weekend manager. I had told my boss that it was my birthday weekend and didn't want to be disturbed, so I'd asked her to be on call over the weekend. She'd agreed, but hadn't liked it. I'm on call three weekends out of each month. Even though I am the director of operations, I still get a lot of the shit jobs my bosses don't want to do. My paycheck is decent, and I usually receive a good Christmas bonus from corporate, not from my immediate supervisor.

My personal cell phone rang in the middle of the day, which was unusual. Everyone knew not to call me during work because I was always so busy. I didn't recognize the number on the caller ID, but I answered it anyway. Somewhere in my mind, I was hoping it was Mark.

I hit the answer icon. "Hello," I said. No one answered. "Hello," I stated again.

"Hi, this is Mark," he said nervously.

"Hello, how are you?" I replied.

"I was wondering if you'd like to join me for a Clippers basketball game. My boss has season tickets but can't attend their next home game. So, would you like to come?" he asked.

The last thing I wanted was to get involved with a married man, especially with someone who had a wife like his. But I rarely did things that were good for me. With much excitement and knowing that I should say an unambiguous no, I said, "I'd love to go."

Mostly, I was thinking about having sex with him again. But maybe not as rough next time. However, I definitely needed to talk to him about not kissing. I love kissing. I could spend hours kissing.

4

Chapter Four

We met at one of the stadium entrances. Mark extended his hand to shake mine.

"It's good to see you," I said.

I was skeptical about why he wanted to see me again after he said nothing would happen between us.

"Where does your wife think you are tonight?" I asked.

"I told her I was going to a game with a friend from work."

"You didn't tell her it was me?" I asked.

"No," Mark answered.

We got a couple of beers and dogs and enjoyed the game. Watching Mark was like watching a little kid. He was jumping up and down, yelling at the players and referees on the court. I could see him relaxing as the night went on. I think the person I saw him become during the game was the real him. His guard was coming down as he forgot about his reality at home. But, during the night, little complaints about his wife kept falling out of his mouth.

"My wife hates it when I drink beer, because she says that's why I have a gut. My wife hates it when I yell at the people on the court. My wife hates most everything I do. I hate that," Mark said sadly.

I grinned for a moment, thinking about what he said about his gut.

"I like your belly. It was rubbing my balls when you were fucking me," I whispered into his ear closest to me, so no one could hear what I said.

He froze like a deer in headlights, his mouth hanging open. I slapped him on his knee, which snapped him out of his daze when a player on the Los Angeles Clippers made a free throw. I could tell that he was an unhappy human being. Maybe I was his new outlet, or perhaps he was searching for one, and possibly that outlet Mark was seeking was me. But I'd like to think I was the reason he finally wanted to be with a guy. Then I thought, "Sort of full of yourself, aren't you?" I chuckled.

After the game, I walked Mark to his car. He thanked me for a great night, shook my hand, and said goodnight. He got into his car and drove away. I had a great night, but I was confused about what he wanted from me. Was this a first date?

I received another phone call at work the next day. This time, his voice showed no hesitation.

"Hi, this is Mark. I'm renting my friend's cabin at a lake up north next weekend. It's about a couple of hours away. We can leave Friday night after work and come back Sunday afternoon."

" Just us?" I asked inquisitively.

"Yes, just us," he replied.

The lake we were going to was not in the mountains, so I

knew the weather would be nice for daytime fishing but chillier at night, especially at the beginning of January. Being out on a lake would be an enjoyable getaway, and maybe some good sex.

"I'd love to go," I replied.

"You don't need to bring any fishing gear because there is gear at the cabin," Mark said.

Mark picked me up at my condo around six the following Friday. I told him I could meet him somewhere, but he said picking me up was better because the lake we were going to was in my direction. I was packed for the weekend and standing in front of my condo building when he arrived. Not knowing what to expect from him, I packed the pot and lube into my large backpack, which I used for weekend getaways.

We stopped for dinner about an hour later. There was another thirty-minute drive after eating. I made an attempt to understand why he was pursuing a friendship with me. He kept changing the subject, so I let it go for now.

For the remainder of the drive, Mark told me about all the things to do at the lake. He said there were great hiking trails, kayaking, and swimming. The little boy in him came out to play again. I liked this side of him. Complaints about his wife resurfaced amid all his excitement.

"She hates hiking, she hates fishing, she hates being out in the sun too long, she hates ..."

"Mark," I said firmly, "I'm enjoying our time together, but there's one thing you can't do, and that's complain about your wife." Mark's face went blank.

"You can talk about your kids, work, parents, cousins, but not about your wife," I added.

"I didn't realize I was doing that," Mark replied.

We agreed that if he started complaining about his wife again, I could remind him that his wife was off-limits.

I still hadn't figured out why Mark had invited me to the lake for the weekend; I was afraid to bring up the subject. We arrived at the lake around eight. Lights inside and outside the cabin were on, so we didn't have to stumble in the dark. The cabin was small and situated in a secluded area of the lake, at the tip of one of the channels. It was more rustic-looking and smaller than some of the modern homes built in recent years.

The cabin's front porch had two rocking chairs on one side, with a small square table between them. How much more rustic can you get? The cabin included a living room, two bedrooms, a bathroom, and a kitchen. Mark pointed to the front bedroom for me to take, and he took the back one. I was hoping to share a bedroom with Mark, but I ended up taking the one he indicated. The furniture was old but still in good condition.

After settling into our rooms, we went to the back patio facing the lake. Jackets were necessary because of the cool night air. A fire pit was near the water's edge, surrounded by stone seating. Plenty of firewood was provided, so I started a fire while Mark stayed on the patio for a wider view of the lake.

"The lake has changed so much over the past few years," Mark uttered.

"You've been here before?" I asked Mark as he came closer to the water.

"Yes. I have brought my son here a few times over the years. Roger, my friend who owns the cabin, has been renting it out for years," Mark answered.

"Your girls didn't like to come here?" I asked.

"No. They are like their mother. This is roughing it to their way of thinking. They don't like outdoor things unless it's sports. No fishing, hiking, camping, and no worms for them," Mark chuckled.

Mark didn't sit next to me by the fire; he sat on the stone seat a couple of feet away as the fire kept us both warm. I could see the tension disappearing from his face now that he was far away from home. We sat and talked about hiking early the next morning, before it got too warm out. I watched his face as the fire flickered and ashes rose and floated away over the lake. Mark would look over at me from the corner of his eye. I think he had hoped I wouldn't see him looking at me. I smiled every time he did. He turned his head away quickly each time.

"I haven't been hiking in quite a long time, so I don't want to push myself the first time out," Mark uttered. I smiled at him.

"I used to be more active," he told me for the tenth time.

I have a feeling he wants me to know that he wasn't always a little pudgy. Pudgy or not, I like him.

"Don't worry. We'll take it slow on our hike. I haven't been hiking in a while either, so let's take it easy and enjoy ourselves. There's no rush," I said.

Besides going to the gym before work every morning five days a week, I didn't tell Mark that I also go for a three-mile walk after work three times a week, so our hike would be effortless for me. I saw Mark smile as he mentioned something about what he used to be like. I felt so bad for him. I wanted him to be happy.

"As I told you the other day, you need to take better care of yourself, for you and no one else," I said caringly. Mark grinned.

After a long week at work, we were both exhausted and just wanted to sleep. I wasn't happy that Mark reminded me to sleep in the other bedroom. I was still confused, but I didn't argue.

As I was falling asleep, I heard moans coming from his room. I got out of bed and quietly approached his door. Standing silent at the open door, I saw him masturbating in the moonlight shining through the window. I think he wanted me to hear him because he wasn't being very quiet about what he was doing.

Mark saw me standing there and stopped what he was doing, still holding his dick. I walked to the far side of the bed where he was lying and watched him for a moment. He didn't protest or ask me to leave. He was silent. I didn't try to kiss him, even though I wanted to so much. I was afraid that he would push me away if I tried. I reached down and held his feet, holding them for a moment to gauge his reaction. He didn't say a word; he just looked up at me.

Spreading his legs apart slowly, I smiled. He was still holding his dick. I crawled between his legs with my stomach flat against the bed. I started licking his balls, which he seemed to love two weeks before. Mark had taken a shower before he climbed into bed and smelled so much better than he did the night I met him.

As I licked him, he started to play with himself again. He stroked his dick vigorously. I held on to his hand that he was using to masturbate and quietly asked him to slow down. He did. After a few minutes, I removed his hand from his penis and put my mouth around it. He let out a deep sigh. I took more time sucking him this time. I didn't want to hurry anything. I loved the size and taste of him inside my mouth. I wanted to explore every inch of his penis and balls.

I rolled his penis around in my mouth with my tongue. I gently used my teeth to bite into his foreskin and stretched it out over the head. There is nothing more sensual than an uncut penis to play with. The moans he released from his throat told me he was enjoying himself and that I was doing an excellent job.

I tried to go down to the base, but only got halfway. There was no way ten inches was going down my throat, but it was fun trying. I placed my tongue between the head and his foreskin again, then ran my tongue around the head, which made him abruptly yell that he was going to come. I stopped instantly because I was not ready for him to come just yet. I had a lot more playing around to do.

His body relaxed after I removed my mouth from his penis. He tightened up once again after I stuck the tip of my tongue into the hole at the end of his dick. I kept digging my tongue deeper while creating as much suction as I could as my mouth engulfed the head. I dug deeper until he yelled, "Oh my god." I stopped at once; I still wasn't ready for him to come. Was I torturing him? Well, maybe!

I rolled Mark on his side. With a pillow under my head, lying on my side, I put him back into my mouth. I continued playing with him until he started to push his penis in and out between my lips. He started slowly, but his pace quickly picked up. I could tell he wanted to come. I created a more potent suction around his dick as he fucked my mouth even faster. When he got close to his orgasm, he grabbed my head with both hands to hold it in place. He needed to come. I think he was tired of being tortured. It wasn't long before he filled my mouth. He tasted so ... good.

Mark didn't move a muscle; he let himself go limp inside my mouth. I tightened my lips around his softening penis and swallowed. I didn't want to upset him, so I said nothing. I didn't go back to the other bedroom either. I rolled over, taking my pillow with me to the head of the bed.

"I need to do something before going to sleep," I told Mark.

I leaned over and kissed him on his shoulder. It would have driven me crazy all night if I hadn't kissed him in some way. Before my eyes shut for good that night, I heard him say softly, "Thank you."

"You're welcome," I replied as tears came to my eyes.

I woke up about thirty minutes before Mark. I was accustomed to waking up by five, so I could go to the gym before work. I started the coffee maker before getting into the shower. I was in the other bedroom getting dressed when Mark sleepily stumbled into the bathroom across from the front bedroom. He shut the door behind him. Thirty minutes later, he walked into the kitchen and said softly, "Good morning."

There was no food in the cabin, so all we had was coffee.

"Let's get something to eat after we hike," I said. Mark grinned.

"We need to have an honest conversation about what's going on between us," I told Mark.

He lowered his head, seeming to be a little embarrassed.

"I'm okay with almost anything as long as I know the rules," I added.

I have told many men that I can handle any situation as long as I know what the rules are during our time together. And what they told me had to be the truth. But most men still lied about what they wanted.

"I don't know how to talk about this stuff, and I don't know what I want," Mark replied, frustratedly.

"Maybe it will be easier to talk while hiking," I said.

We took many breaks during our short hike. I think he was attempting something he wasn't ready for because he just wanted to spend time with me. We discussed our likes and dislikes over breakfast the morning after we met, so I have no idea why he chose the most difficult activity. During one of our breaks, we sat on opposite sides of a small tree, backs to each other, and talked.

"At home, my wife is not abusive to me if the kids are around. When the kids are not around, as you saw at dinner, she doesn't treat me very well. And if I argue back, she makes my life a living hell. We try to stay apart as much as we can. She told me if I ever tried to divorce her, she would do her best to destroy me financially and take my kids from me," he continued with a sad tone in his voice. "I love my kids, and I stay just for them."

I sat quietly looking into the sky, and heard nothing from Mark for several minutes. I didn't ask him if he was okay. I wanted to give him time to think.

"She is used to me being gone a lot. I go to work and don't come home until I know the kids are home. We don't have sex anymore, and I sleep in another room. The kids think I sleep in another room because of a sleeping disorder," he uttered.

"Are you okay?" I asked.

"I've never talked to anyone about this stuff before. I keep it inside. Sometimes, I feel like I'm going to explode," Mark said sadly.

I moved to sit in front of him so I could see his reactions. He didn't stop me. I could see by his expressions just how much he loved his kids. He hadn't smiled very often; it was mostly pain I'd seen on his face. But I wanted to see more of his smiles because they are beautiful and sexy. I wanted him to believe that.

"I don't want to get a divorce while the kids are still living at home. She wasn't like this twenty years ago. We once loved each other and had a lot of fun together. But after the kids came along and life became harder, and there wasn't as much play time for us, she became a very angry person, and it was all aimed at me," he continued, completely drained.

"She said she wanted kids, so we had the kids. I helped as much as I could after working all day, but whatever I did never seemed to be enough. I do my best to make sure the kids have everything they need. She is the best mom in the world to the kids, so I don't understand where her anger is coming from, and she has never shared it with me," he added.

I knew we had a lot more to discuss, but I didn't want to rush him. I could see the despair on his face from sharing so much.

After our hike, we were both extremely hungry. We went to a downtown diner for an early lunch or late breakfast. Small-town diners are the best. The food tastes homemade, and the service is always friendly. We sat in a corner booth, and the server had a Southern accent. She was young, tiny, and full of energy, with long black hair tied back in a ponytail. She didn't wear much makeup, and she didn't need to. She was one of those women who look pretty without it.

"What can I get you, boys, today?" she exclaimed with a smile.

"We have a great open-faced turkey sandwich with gravy and mashed potatoes. It's our lunch special today. And, oh yes, and pie for dessert. How about it, boys?" she added, guiding us to the correct answer.

Mark and I grinned at each other and shook our heads in acknowledgment.

"You boys are so easy," she said, as she turned and walked away just as quickly as she had walked up to our table.

After lunch, we stopped at the grocery store to buy steaks

and corn on the cob to grill for dinner. We were so full after lunch that we decided to take a nap. Returning to the cabin, we put the food in the fridge, we got undressed down to our underwear, crawled into the same bed, and fell asleep quickly. Mark stayed on his side of the bed, and I was on mine. A little more than an hour later, we woke. Mark was wrapped around my backside with a boner pressing against me. He let go of me quickly when he realized where he was. I didn't say anything because he needs to figure out by himself just what he wants from me.

Besides, I needed to see if I could handle all this. It took me long enough—years, in fact—to admit or figure out who I was. It's tougher for some people than others. Some guys quickly say, "Yes, I'm gay," and others struggle. It was a major battle for me, especially during my teenage years and when I was in the Navy. It's not that I hate who I am or hate that I'm attracted to men; it's how people have treated me that I hate. Some, not all, straight people hate me because I'm gay, and some gay people, not all, tell me I'm not gay enough to be one of them. I am so confused.

When I got up from my nap, I splashed water on my face and brushed my teeth. I stepped out onto the back porch overlooking the lake. I watched people in boats and kids splashing in the water. I still couldn't believe the beautiful weather we were having for January. I love sunshine. That's why I stayed in Southern California after I left the Navy. My mood always improved when the sun was shining. If the weather remained dark and gloomy for long periods, my mood would plummet, and I could fall into a deep depression.

When Mark joined me on the porch, he still looked a little sleepy. I think he was having an awkward moment from waking up, pressed against my backside. He looked downward at the porch, not saying anything coherent. I didn't bother asking him what he said. I was starting to get tired of his mixed messages. I considered the possibility that he might never be able to come to terms with who he truly is.

We took the fishing poles and bait to the pier to fish, rather than taking the small boat into the middle of the lake. The cabin came with a small fishing boat, so we would not have to rent one. The pier was fine for us. A large red oak tree stood tall near the dock, providing us with shade. A light breeze blew Mark's hat off his head and onto the pier. I picked it up and handed it back to him. He smiled at me, and I pressed my lips together. We sat there for an hour or so and didn't catch anything. Sometimes, I'm okay when I don't catch any fish. For me, it's very relaxing to have my fishing pole in my hand. I would lift my pole out of the water, check the bait, and make another cast. Then I would turn the reel's crank to take the slack out of the line, sit back, and wait. We didn't talk much while we fished, which I didn't mind. I love the quiet. I looked over at Mark from time to time, hoping that he was going to fuck me before the weekend was over.

We went back to the porch, sat rocking in our chairs, and mainly talked about sports. We gradually returned to the subject of what he was looking for from me. He turned his chair away from me as we spoke, so he didn't have to look at me.

"I like being around you. I have a strong urge to be near you, but I have never felt this for a guy before," Mark said hesitantly.

I could tell from Mark's voice that this conversation was stressing him out.

"Enough talking for now, let's go do something fun," I told

him.

"Before we stop talking, I'd like to say one more thing if that's okay," he said softly.

I sat quietly as I heard him take a deep breath.

"If nothing else, I would like to become good friends, someone that I can talk to about things, someone I could go places with," he uttered.

That's what he said he wanted more than anything from me. I told him that I also needed to say something.

"Are you also looking for a friend with benefits?" I exclaimed bluntly.

Mark's eyes opened wide as he took an intense breath.

"You've made it very clear that you do, even if you're still in denial about it," I stated matter-of-factly.

"Maybe," he said.

A moment of hope struck me hard, along with a moment of bravery.

"Then you're going to have to get past the no-kissing thing. I like romance, and that includes a lot of kissing," I added.

Mark didn't reply.

5

Chapter Five

We went to a local sports bar downtown and had a couple of beers. A Clippers game was on TV when we arrived. Mark yelled at the TV just as much as he had at the stadium. We arrived halfway through the game. After two beers, the game was over. I suppose I'm a bit of a silent yeller. Inside my head, I was shouting the same things Mark was yelling aloud. I was trying not to admit it, but as I watched Mark yelling at the TV and having a good time, I felt a tug on my heartstrings.

The tavern was in the heart of town, where people strolled the streets, exploring shops along the way. This lake town was one of many in Southern California and popular among weekend visitors. There was always a chance of bumping into someone you knew. The game was over, and we were growing hungry. We headed back to Mark's car, which was parked about a hundred feet from the tavern.

"If I run into someone I know, especially someone my wife

knows, and if they ask, we work together," Mark told me.

"If that happens, I'm not lying. You answer for me," I responded. Mark frowned.

At that moment, I felt like the other woman. I didn't like that feeling. I've never gone out with a gay man who had a partner I knew of, but here I was with a married man. Why didn't I see the two as the same? In gay life, you must ask the direct question before going on a date, because there are so many men who have open relationships or cheat.

Mark pulled into our parking spot in front of the cabin. We remained silent during the ride back, still tense from our previous conversation. I walked through the front door and immediately out the back door. Mark stopped in the kitchen, pulled out the steaks, corn, and salad ingredients from the refrigerator.

"I'll light the charcoal," I said, somewhat grumpily from the rear patio.

"Are you okay?" Mark asked.

"I'm a little upset," I replied.

I went back into the cabin to help Mark prepare dinner. He had the corn with the husk still on, soaking in water to grill. I placed the steaks on a platter and seasoned them. Mark was being playful with me, which was unusual. You know what I mean. He was bumping into me while I was working at the counter, chopping vegetables for the salad, and coming up behind me to tickle me. Was he trying to make up with me for what he said earlier? I thought he almost kissed me on the cheek, but pulled away at the last second. He kissed me on my cheek the night we met, but I guess back then, it was him messing around, wanting some pot. But if he kissed me now, that would mean something different. Maybe it was the two beers we drank at the tavern. You know the old saying: Two beers turn any man gay.

I had never seen that happen. I wish it had, but it never did.

I did have a bad crush on a straight male co-worker once when I was younger; he knew I was gay. He started asking me to do things with him, like going to baseball games and hanging out at the beach near his apartment in Santa Monica. We always had fun. I even thought he was flirting with me from time to time. He was very touchy-feely. I was confused. I had been out of the closet for only two years at the time.

He asked me to go to Santa Barbara with him for the day one Sunday. We left at six in the morning and wouldn't return until well after dark. During the hour-and-a-half drive, we told jokes, sang along to the country music on the radio, and talked about his family vacation to the Rocky Mountains.

Around noon, we had a few beers and a sandwich at the tavern across from the beach. We spent an hour playing frisbee to let our food settle, then spent half an hour body surfing. The waves were excellent. The water was sandy because of the strong undercurrent, and we had a lot of sand in our suits.

"Let's go into one of the private changing shacks on the beach to get rid of the sand," he said.

I had just shut the door to the shack when he dropped his trunks to his ankles and stepped out of them. I was frozen, unable to move, staring at him. He was slender and tall. He turned to face me and gave me a full-frontal view as he brushed off all the sand from his crotch. I finally got to see the goods. He wasn't hiding anything from me. I wanted to reach out and touch him so badly, but I didn't want a fist in my face if I was wrong. Still, I wondered why he turned to give me a full-frontal, knowing I would look at him.

He finished brushing off the sand from his crotch and upper thighs, and then shook out his trunks. He stepped back into them, pulled them up, and said, "Are you done yet? Let's go."

He had to know that I was staring at him because he had to ask me the same question twice before I heard him. "Are you done yet?" he asked again.

He had no expression on his face, just a blank stare.

"I still have to get rid of my sand," I'd said.

"I'll wait outside," he'd replied.

I guess he didn't want to see my stuff. So, a few beers don't make a straight man gay.

On our drive home to his apartment in Santa Monica, where my car was parked, he told me about his new girlfriend, whom he had met about two months ago. He said he didn't say anything earlier because he didn't know for sure if he was going to keep seeing her. I hoped it didn't show on my face, but as he talked about his new girlfriend, I could barely breathe. After he dropped me off at my car, I never saw him again except at work. We rarely spoke to each other after that, except for work-related matters.

Mark and I like our steaks the same way, medium-rare. We cooked the corn in its husk on the grill. With a dinner salad as a side loaded with vegetables, we sat down to eat. I talked about my job to keep Mark from complaining about his wife. Several times throughout the day, I had to remind him that his wife was off-limits.

After dinner, we sat by the fire pit to stay warm while watching the sun set over the lake. This time, Mark and I sat on the same stone seat, but he made sure there was space between us. Mark wanted to show me something on the lake. He placed his hand on my knee to get my attention and kept it there for several minutes. I didn't say anything about it because I didn't want him to pull away. I felt as if he was becoming more comfortable with me, or maybe he didn't realize what he was doing, but I hoped he did.

"Did you bring any pot with you?" he asked softly. "I love listening to all the animal noises around the lake when I'm stoned."

My first thought was that I was going to get laid tonight, which made me smile big.

"That sounds like fun," I said. "Yes, I brought some pot. I'll go get it."

We moved to the back porch of the cabin to relax in the patio chairs, rocking gently as we smoked and watched the fire pit burn out for the night.

"I love this pot," Mark chuckled. I smiled.

After hiking, a big dinner, and a couple of beers and pot, I was soon snoozing in my chair.

Mark woke me up and said, "Let's go to bed."

We undressed and stumbled our way to the bathroom for the last time of the night. I waited for him to finish so I could have a private moment alone. Not knowing if anything would happen, I needed to make sure I was properly prepared.

I thought Mark was already asleep when I looked into his bedroom. So I crawled in on the other side of him and pulled a sheet over me. He didn't say anything, so I stayed. We were both naked. Mark had nothing covering him, so I took one last look at his large penis for the night. I thought about putting it in my mouth, but decided not to. I rolled onto my stomach, and I could feel sleep overtaking me.

Not quite asleep, I felt my sheet being pulled off me. Mark was moving very softly as if he was sneaking up on me for an attack. He must have brought his own lube because he was greasing up my hole. I was still very stoned from the last hit of pot we took about thirty minutes before bed. I didn't move at all as he applied lube to my butt. I wanted to see what he was going to do. He climbed slowly on top of me, and I felt the head of his dick in the crack of my butt. I surprised him when I said, "This is not *Brokeback Mountain*. You ask before you enter."

Mark quickly jumped back to his side of the bed. He started apologizing in a panicked tone.

I told him to relax and that I was not mad.

"I know you're confused about what you want. But you can tell me anything. You don't have to be afraid of how you are feeling," I said, caringly.

"When I try to say something, my throat swells shut. I wanted to ask you, but I was hoping you would have said something," Mark said, stumbling over his words.

"Maybe I should have, but I was afraid that I would scare you away," I added.

Mark looked like he wanted to speak, but no words came out.

"Why were you so confident the night we met, but not tonight?" I asked.

"Something is different now. At the dance club, thoughts about sex were swirling in my head, but I wasn't going to do anything about them. But after we smoked your strong pot, nothing was going to stop me. And I didn't know you then like I do now," Mark uttered.

My heart was beating fast. Was he attempting to tell me he liked me?

"I want to have sex with you more than I want to admit," Mark said softly.

"Well, from this moment on, it has to start with a kiss. I love kissing. You kissed me on my cheek the night we met, so why not my lips?" I asked him.

Mark paused to gather his thoughts.

"I've never kissed a man on the lips before. And I've never wanted to until now," he said.

"So, you have thought about kissing me?" I asked as I moved closer to him.

"Yes," he said hesitantly.

"Well, you have had your dick in my ass and my mouth. Kissing is much simpler," I told him with a chuckle.

I placed my hand on his shoulder to pull myself nearer. I could feel his body tense at my touch.

"Relax," I said softly. "This won't hurt. You liked my mouth on your penis, and you'll also like it on your lips."

I first kissed him on his cheek, and then I moved to his neck. He seemed to be okay so far. He didn't pull away from me.

"Are you okay with me kissing you?" I asked.

"Yes," he replied nervously.

My lips met his, and the kiss lasted several seconds. I felt him lean into the kiss. He pulled back from me and turned on the dim light on the nightstand.

"Why did you do that?" I asked.

"I wanted to see your face," he replied. I smiled.

He leaned in and kissed me back.

"I don't know why I was so terrified of kissing you. I enjoyed it," he said.

"The first kiss can be terrifying. I knew I wanted to kiss a guy, but I was taught that anything with a guy was wrong. My father wouldn't even hug me as a kid. I felt sick the first time I kissed a man. But luckily, my first time was with a really nice guy. He was also my first for anal sex that same night. I fought being gay for as long as I could. So when I decided not to be so afraid anymore, I made the decision to find out what I liked and what I didn't like," I explained.

We lay side by side on the bed, facing each other, and kissed. A tear rolled down his cheek as he looked into my eyes. I brushed the tear away with my thumb and smiled. I didn't ask about the tear because I was afraid it would make him pull away, and he had just started to open up.

I asked Mark to lie on his back and told him to speak up if I did anything he didn't like, and I would stop. I kissed him slowly from his head to his toes and then halfway back up again. It was hard to kiss a place that didn't have any hair, but telling him he needed a good trimming would have spoiled the mood. He was one hairy man. I pulled myself up to lie on top of him, looking into his eyes. He smiled and kissed me again. I told him it was now his turn to do what he wanted to me, or he could tell me what to do.

"Can I get inside you?" he asked.

Mark had just gotten comfortable with kissing me, so maybe it would take a little longer before he was ready to put his mouth on any of my body parts.

"Tell me what position you want me in," I said.

"On your back so I can look at you," he asked softly.

I rolled over, and he eagerly edged himself between my legs.

"Would you wrap your legs around me?" he asked.

I smiled, and he smiled back.

I grabbed the lube from the nightstand and put some in his hand. He grinned. Mark seemed more relaxed now that we'd talked. He knew where to put the lube, but didn't know where to wipe off his hands. I laughed. He looked puzzled.

"Usually, men keep extra towels nearby to wipe the lube off

their hands after applying it," I explained.

I saw my T-shirt within reach, so I grabbed it and told him to wipe his hands on it. I was having so much fun watching him fumble around.

"Let me help," I said.

I pulled his face toward mine and kissed him. He relaxed and smiled. I took his penis and placed it at my hole and told him to push forward. He slid right in, and a smile came to his face. Once inside me, he moved slowly until he was tight against me. A gasp of air entered my lungs. I loved the feeling of him filling up my backside. A large penis inside me is like shooting a drug into me. Every nerve in my body becomes activated.

"Did you mean it when you said you like it when my belly rubs your balls?" he asked, chuckling.

"Yes, I do." I giggled.

Mark didn't go crazy on my ass like he did on our first night. He moved slowly and gently. He found spots inside me that drove me crazy. Moans roared out of me. He laughed when I made them. He kept leaning in and giving me kisses. Some of them were quick, and others lasted several seconds. He found another spot inside me that made my body shake and shiver. He kept doing it until I said I could no longer take it. He laughed.

"You're evil," I stated.

"I can be." He chuckled. The little boy in him was coming out to play again. His walls were coming down, I hoped.

I played with my penis while he was inside me. I stroked my shaft in tempo with his movements. I held him tight with my legs as he moved. His belly massaged my balls.

"I want to come just before you do. So give me a warning if you can. And don't come inside me this time. I want you to pull out in time so you can shoot onto my stomach. I want to watch you come, and see the expression on your face," I said breathlessly. He laughed.

"I'm getting close," Mark grunted.

I can make myself come quickly if I play with just the head of my dick. Within seconds after I came, he pulled out and shot one long stream from my belly button to my chin. I will never know how this man produces so much sperm. The amount that came out of him was incredible. I laughed. His face crinkled up when he came. I laughed again.

"Why are you laughing?" Mark asked, a little worried.

"Because you're so cute when you come," I replied.

"I'm not cute," he said gruffly.

I thought for a moment.

"No, no, you're not," I responded. Mark looked so sad. "You're not cute. You're absolutely adorable," I uttered caringly.

He smiled and kissed me. I was getting emotional, and my eyes welled up with tears. All I wanted was to see Mark happy.

We were a little sticky—actually, quite sticky. Mark grabbed the T-shirt he had used earlier and wiped us off. He lay down next to me, facing me, kissed me, and we fell asleep within seconds.

It was nearly eight a.m. when we woke up, but this morning was different. Mark was pressed against my backside. He didn't pull away; he squeezed me a little tighter. I loved the feeling of him tight against me. We got out of bed for a morning pee, brushed our teeth, and got back into bed. Mark was becoming the aggressor. He pulled me closer to him and kissed me. But not just a kiss—there was tongue in play now. Not a lot, but it was a good start.

"Can I ask you something?" Mark uttered softly.

"Sure, you can ask me anything," I replied kindly.

"I know we have to head back home this morning, so time is short, but ... can we have a quickie to start the day?" Mark chuckled.

"Of course," I said, "Yes, please."

I made sure I was ready for him before I got back into bed, just in case he asked. I love morning sex. When he said a quickie, he meant a quickie—because after a few minutes, I had my orgasm, and he had his as he pulled out of me and shot from my belly button to my chin. He grinned widely as if to say, "See what I did?" And we were up and into the shower.

This time in the shower, Mark took the washcloth, put soap on it, and began washing me from head to toe. He was very playful with me as he washed. He was playing with my penis as he stood in front of me and gave me a few wonderful kisses. The entire time he was kissing me, my brain was screaming, He's touching my dick, he's touching my dick. This is a big deal. I grabbed his face with both hands and kissed him hard. By the smile on his face, I think he knew why I kissed him so hard.

Mark rinsed me off with the handheld shower head and spent a few extra minutes between my legs getting rid of all the soap suds. A kiss brought out a whole new side of him. I felt my attraction towards him grow stronger, and I knew what that feeling meant to me. I started to get a little emotional, so I stuck my head under the shower so he would not see the tears coming from my eyes.

I got out of the shower while Mark finished washing himself. I was dressed by the time he came into the bedroom. I loved looking at him naked. I loved his little potbelly, and I loved watching his big dick swing like an elephant's trunk as he walked into the bedroom.

"Can I ask you something?" Mark mumbled.

"Sure. But please stop asking me if you can ask me something. Just ask me. You're safe with me," I said caringly.

"Would you put my dick in your mouth just for a moment, please?" He grinned.

I smiled, got down on my knees, and put it in my mouth. I was amazed at how quickly he got hard. He stepped back, pulling it out of my mouth after a few minutes. He looked down at me and smiled.

"There are things you can do with a man that you can't do with a woman," he stated.

"Yes, Mark ... you are correct," I chuckled.

We needed to get back to the city by mid-afternoon, so we packed up the car and headed to the diner for a late breakfast before hitting the road. We got the same young lady with the Southern accent that we had the day before. As we walked in the front door of the diner, she said, "Couldn't live without me, could you boys? Sit down, and I will be right with you."

We sat in the same booth we had occupied previously. We didn't know what we wanted to eat, and I don't think she likes it when people take a long time deciding. Just like when we came for lunch, she said, "How about I bring you both a big breakfast that has a little bit of everything?"

We both answered, "Sounds good."

"How do you want your eggs, sweeties?" she asked.

"Over easy, please," we both replied.

After a couple of cups of coffee and a big breakfast that could have served a family of four, we were on our way home. It's good to get an early start on a Sunday because traffic is a nightmare by late afternoon, no matter where you are traveling to or from. Even driving from North Hollywood, where I lived, to Mark's house forty-five minutes away can be a nightmare on a Sunday afternoon.

Mark wanted to be home by four because he promised his two girls that he would run soccer drills with them. We got to my condo at two thirty. He wanted to come up for a minute, but I was afraid it would turn into hours, not minutes, and I didn't want to be the reason he showed up late for his girls. He knew I was right, so he remained in his car while I got my bag out of the trunk and set it on the curb.

No one knew Mark in my neighborhood, so I asked him for a kiss goodbye, but he hesitated. I told him that no one could see us. I leaned in for a quick kiss. He looked stunned. I told him to drive safely, and I couldn't wait to see him again. I don't know exactly what it was, but I think reality sank in for him as his face shifted from a smile to a vacant expression. The look on his face said it all. My gut told me I would never see him again.

He waited until I got inside my building before he drove away. I could see him through the front window. He waved to me as he pulled away from the curb with that blank look still on his face. I waved back. I felt sad and lonely as he drove off.

For the remainder of the day, I couldn't lose the dreaded feeling that I might never see Mark again. I went for a long walk after dinner to shake off the horrible feeling, but it didn't work. I stared at my phone while sitting on my sofa, thinking that I should text him to make sure he got home okay, but I chickened out. Around nine p.m., exhausted from the weekend, I knew I wouldn't be able to sleep no matter how tired I was, so I took a hit of pot. My pot always makes me horny, so I grabbed my dildo from its hiding place under the underwear in my dresser, took the lube from the nightstand, and fifteen minutes later, I was taking a hot shower, so I would be nice and clean before climbing into my freshly made bed with clean sheets.

6

Chapter Six

I expected Mark to call on Monday morning, but there was no call. A few more days went by, and I hadn't heard from him. I wasn't sure whether I was relieved or sad, but my heart felt as if it were breaking just a little. We had a great weekend together, or at least the end of it was. My feelings for him grew stronger, and I believe they did for him as well.

Was I falling for another man who might bring more chaos into my life, or could he be the one to help fix it? He carried so much negativity that I believed it would eventually tear us apart. Also, did I want to date a man who was married to a woman when I didn't want to date a man married to another man?

But if I was honest with myself, I fell hard for Mark, and I don't know why. Maybe I believed I didn't deserve anything better than a dysfunctional relationship. Living in secrecy for a few years until he could get a divorce after his kids were fully grown would have been very difficult. And why was I thinking of forever after only two weeks? How desperate was I? Plus, what if his wife kept her promise and ruined him financially—leaving us to live on my paycheck alone? I was making a good income, but by California standards, my paycheck was just above average. It had taken me a long time to accept who I am, and I didn't want to go back into the closet for anyone. Still, I was hurting without him.

By the time I got home from work on Thursday evening, I was a complete wreck. I could hardly eat, drink, or sleep. I wasn't going to the gym or taking walks after dinner, which I loved. The only thing that stayed the same was my work. I never let anything interfere with it. I had too many people counting on me, and I never let them see my vulnerable side. My next-door neighbor, a retired school teacher, sixty-eight years old, and as nosy as can be—which I loved, and maybe the only person who didn't judge me—knocked on my front door.

"What's going on?" she bellowed as I opened my front door.

I actually jumped, she was so loud. Plus, I was stoned. That was the only way I was coping.

"Okay, Alex. What's wrong? You're not going to the gym, you're not sleeping — because you look like crap — and you're stoned at seven o'clock," she said as she pushed her way into my condo carrying a tray full of her homemade chicken parmesan, a side of spaghetti and meatballs, an antipasto salad, and a large container of cannoli that would last me for four days, which she knew was my favorite.

"Nothing," I replied sadly.

"Don't give me that nonsense, young man. This five-foot-two Italian knows when you're lying to her. So tell me what's going on?"

I didn't get a chance to say anything before she barked at me again.

"But first, you need to eat something. Food makes everything better, you'll see. It always has in the past when I fed you, and we always got you back on track, didn't we?" Marie stated.

Marie and I had lived next door to each other for ten years since I bought my condo. But we didn't start talking regularly until after her husband died two years ago of a heart attack. She was eighteen when she met her husband, Peter, ten years older than her, while he was on vacation with friends in Rome. She was the cutest little thing—well, not so little now. She might be short, but she's wide, with gray hair to her shoulders, hazel eyes, and puffy cheeks. I adore her. Why didn't I have a mom like her instead of the angry woman who gave birth to me?

I shut my front door, and she told me to sit at my dining room table. I always obeyed her; there wasn't an option. She went into the kitchen and served me a generous amount of food on a plate. She placed it in front of me and told me to eat everything, or there would be no cannoli.

"Yes, ma'am," I replied.

She placed a Diet Pepsi in front of me and said pointedly, "Tell me what's going on, sweetheart. You know I'm here for you."

"Tell me how you are first," I said, placing a forkful of food in my mouth. "We haven't talked since you made me dinner just before my birthday," I added, wanting to change the subject.

"Don't talk with your mouth full, sweetie, and that's not going to work this time, trying to change the subject," she said. "You need to talk about what's going on! You're stressed out. I can tell."

"Did you used to be a therapist?" I asked.

"No! I am a mother! An Italian mother! I'm pushy, and I always get my way. Ask my three boys. We talk about everything in their lives, and nothing is off-limits, even sex. They make fun of me and call me Dr. Ruth," she said with a chuckle. "And one of my boys is gay—you've met him. He met his boyfriend in college, and they've been together ever since, so I've never had to discuss his sexual adventures like the ones you've had. But, like I said, I am here for you, so talk. And yes, you need to make an appointment with your therapist," she added firmly.

I couldn't help but laugh. She is amazing.

"Well, this is going to be a wet one. So, can we talk after I get done eating? I don't want to cry over your delicious food," I said.

After eating more food than I should have, mostly because I was stoned and had the munchies, we sat on the sofa and talked for the next two hours. I told her every detail of what had happened since my birthday—the expressions on her face after certain comments were priceless. But every time her eyes widened, she squeezed my hand and never made a negative comment.

The one thing I've never told Marie, and probably never will, is how depressed I feel sometimes and how dark thoughts race through my mind—my feelings of worthlessness, self-hatred, and thoughts of harming myself. However, I believe she knows how I feel without me having to say it out loud because she has politely brought it up during our conversations.

"I hear about people hurting themselves all the time, and I don't ever want things to get so bad that you think of doing something like that," she would say with tears in her eyes. "That would hurt me so deeply."

"I would never do that to you," I'd answer kindly. But I wasn't sure I could keep my promise to her. Most nights before I would fall asleep, I would think, 'Please don't wake up tomorrow morning.'

"Now make that appointment with your therapist for tomorrow. Promise me," she said as she stood up from the living room sofa to leave.

"I promise," I replied.

As soon as Marie left, I called and left a voice mail for my therapist.

At ten the next morning, while I was at work, my cell phone rang with the tone I had set for her, 'I Love Rock 'n Roll' by Joan Jett and the Blackhearts. She was five foot eight, slender, with dishwater blonde hair and greenish hazel eyes. She identified as bisexual.

"Doctor Smith," I said instead of hello.

"Your voice mail sounded urgent. What can I help you with?" she asked.

"I'm at one of those points where I'm having bad thoughts," I said anxiously. "Can I see you tonight?"

"Let me look at my schedule ... How about seven thirty? You'll be my last appointment. Does that work?" she replied.

"That's great, Doc, see you then," I responded excitedly.

Marie had helped me so much, but knowing that I was going to talk with Dr. Smith made my whole body relax. She always cuts straight to the point. She wasn't going to tolerate my BS or wait for me to tell her what I was dealing with. I loved that about her. It had taken me years to find the right therapist, and that was the key to handling emotional issues. Even though she has helped me through tough times, she hasn't been able to help me love or care for myself; no therapist had been able to do that over the previous ten years. Those moments of self-love had been brief.

Just like I had when talking to Marie last night, I shared with Dr. Smith every detail of my life since my birthday. I cried at some points, and we laughed through others. She sat quietly listening as I rambled because she knows how easily I lose my train of thought. I couldn't believe those first words out of her mouth, but that's what I loved about her.

"You like your big dick, don't you?" she said, laughing. I had to laugh along with her.

"And you like your drama, too," she said bluntly.

I stopped laughing and made a face like an angry five-year-old. These were the times I didn't like her much, when she cut right through my crap. But I also loved that about her. I'm fickle, what can I say?

"Are you sure it's not his big dick and his drama you fell for? What does he have to offer you if not more crap? You bring enough drama into your own relationships. So why are you looking for more?" she stated, gazing into my eyes with conviction.

My heart was pounding so hard that my chest ached. I wanted to cry to make her feel sorry for me, but she would call me out on it. She only pointed out things she knew she could quickly help me understand. I needed to figure things out fast so I could get those thoughts of harming myself out of my head. I knew that by the time I left her office, I would be feeling better because she wouldn't let me go unless I was more stable.

"Name one thing about this man that's going to improve your life?" she asked.

I sat quietly for a few moments, trying to figure out how to answer.

"Nothing," I said, defeated.

"Do you mean it, or are you telling me what you think I want to hear?" Dr. Smith asked caringly.

"I mean it," I answered. "I really do." I wiped a few tears from my eyes.

I wasn't really sure whether I was telling her the truth.

"Mark is a man who doesn't love himself. Do you understand that?" she asked.

"Yes, I know that," I said, releasing a deep sigh.

"He is experiencing what many closeted men go through. A man in his fifties who has hidden his true self for so long, and the stress, anxiety, loneliness, depression, and fear of damaging his relationships with his wife, children, and friends are overwhelming for him. It might seem small compared with everything else I mentioned, but at fifty, he's wondering whether he is still desirable."

I sat quietly, lost in thought for a moment.

"Every time I paid Mark a compliment, like how sexy or cute I thought he was, those comments upset him the most. I never thought of that before," I said, exhaling hard.

I was so exhausted after two hours of talking with Dr. Smith, but I also felt a lot better.

"You fell for Mark because he filled a void temporarily. You were lonely on your birthday. And now that he's gone, you feel that void again, and you want to fill it," she said pointedly.

I sat silently, waiting for her to speak again.

"So over the next few weeks, I want to work with you on finding a good person to bring into your life, someone who will love you because you're a good person, and they will see that," she stated, caringly.

"You know I hate you, don't you?" I said.

"Good. Then I know I am doing my job," she replied, laughing.

We sat quietly staring at each other with blank faces until she grinned.

"Is Marie keeping an eye on you?" Dr. Smith asked.

"Yes. She was worried about me because she noticed my daily routine had changed dramatically. She brought me dinner last night, and we talked and cried—well, I cried. She's a tough old bird. I don't know what I'd do without her," I said.

"You say people don't love you, but she does. Why can't you believe that?" Dr. Smith wondered.

"Because when anyone says they love you, they will turn around and hurt you," I answered, my chest tightening.

"Well, we'll work on that," she said, chuckling. "Now, go home. It's Friday night. Make plans for the weekend. Don't sit at home dwelling on something you know isn't good for you. Get outside. Go hiking or exercise—something you love. Go shopping. You enjoy that. Visit the antique shops in Orange County, and go to your favorite Cuban restaurant that serves fried plantains. And I will see you Tuesday at seven," she added as she pushed me out the door.

On my drive home, many thoughts raced through my mind. I knew Dr. Smith was right about Mark. He was bad for me; he's not a bad person, but he has a lot of things to work on in his life. Nevertheless, I kept clinging to my need for him.

I made a weekend plan just as Dr. Smith instructed, right after I entered my condo. I needed to stay as busy as possible to keep my mind off Mark. Was Dr. Smith right when she said I was more attracted to Mark's big dick than I was to Mark? Was he filling the void of feeling lonely on my birthday? Could I be that—what's the word I'm looking for—childish, self-centered, screwed-up, emotionally disturbed, needy, or all of the above? I'm such a loser. And I decided to do as she told me just before I left her office.

"*Don't use sex as your coping mechanism. Stay away from the bars. Another big dick isn't going to replace your feelings for Mark. And no more unprotected sex!*" I heard her voice echo in my head.

After a solid ten hours of sleep, which I think was due to complete exhaustion, I woke up to a gentle knock on my front door. My little Italian neighbor, smiling, looked up at me as I opened the door, holding a plate of freshly baked biscotti—some covered in chocolate, some plain.

"How are you today?" she asked. "Here are some biscotti I made for you to enjoy with your coffee."

"Would you like to join me?" I replied.

"No, I'm off to have breakfast with my son, Johnny, and his partner, Gabriel. They recently returned from visiting our family in Italy, and they have many pictures to show me," she answered.

"How wonderful. I'd love to see Italy someday. Enjoy your visit with them," I said, smiling.

"I can tell you're feeling better this morning. Your smile tells me everything. Do you have plans for today?" she asked.

"Yes. I'm antique shopping and having lunch in Orange County. Then I'm going to the gym in the late afternoon, picking up a couple of DVDs I've been wanting to watch, and having dinner at the café around the corner. And tomorrow I'm going for a long hike," I said, still smiling.

"Good. Getting out and about will do you some good," she said as she grabbed my shirt collar and pulled me toward her to kiss my cheek.

"Now, I'm off to my son's house. If you need me, I'll be home around three. Remember, I do not have a cell phone. My son wants me to get one, but I don't like those things," she added.

I shut the door and walked into the kitchen to turn on the coffee maker I had prepared the night before, so all I had to do was turn it on. I thought about my last morning with Mark and our quickie, so I looked toward the bathroom, needing to take a shower, then back to bed, where my dildo and lube were lying on my nightstand. Nothing wrong with a fast one to start my day, I thought. So off with my robe and boxers, and I jumped back into bed.

On Monday morning, I kept waiting for my phone to ring. It didn't ring on Tuesday either. I kept my appointment with Dr. Smith at seven p.m.

"Good job on planning a fun weekend. And I am especially proud of you for not going to the bars to find sex," she said, enthusiastically.

We reviewed everything we had discussed in our previous session. I was feeling much better by the end of this session, after she once again pointed out to me why Mark was bad for me. She gave me more things to work on before our next appointment. She always gave me homework because, as she likes to say, it takes a long time to teach old dogs new tricks.

I get so angry with myself because I always end up in the same place—hurt and desperate to be loved. If Mark wanted to come out of the closet on our birthdays, why didn't he ask me questions about sex with a man before using me like a cheap hooker? I know he'd told me on our last day together that things were different then, but he could have hurt me with his big dick if I had been inexperienced with something that large, and I've never cared about anyone so little that I'd want to hurt them like he could have hurt me. But I also allowed him to hurt me; I permitted him to treat me like a hooker when I told him he could do whatever he wanted to me. That felt like love to me. Why can't I care about myself? Why do I think I need someone to love me first before I can love myself?

7

Chapter Seven

It's been several weeks since I'd last seen Mark. Some friends asked me to go dancing with them because they wanted to make up for not celebrating my birthday with me. People don't often call me to spend an evening together, so I wasn't going to turn them down. We were heading to Oil Can Harry's, the same dance club I had taken Mark to on our birthdays.

The club was crowded as usual for a Saturday night. The younger crowd that always paid attention to me kept trying to get me onto the dance floor, but I was not in the mood. I felt sad most of the night. I kept looking around, waiting for Mark to be somewhere in the crowd, but I never saw him. And why would he be there? He wasn't gay. He was probably at home with his wife and kids. I worried that everything he told me about never being with a guy before was a lie.

"Did I make a mistake when I had unprotected sex with him?" I said aloud to myself.

The man standing next to me, as I was leaning against the stage at the front of the club, asked, "Did you say something to me?"

I looked bewildered when he spoke.

"No, sorry. I was thinking out loud." He smiled and turned away from me.

But I guess I caught someone's attention because a man with a deep voice came over and asked, "Are you looking for someone?"

I quickly turned to my side, thinking that it was Mark. My smile disappeared promptly as I turned.

"Hi, my name is John. I've been watching you look around the club, trying to find someone, but not locating them. Would I do?"

The man had a great smile.

"No, no, thank you," I said abruptly. He was still smiling at me even though I was a little rude.

"Sorry, I didn't mean to sound so harsh," I said softly.

He kept smiling at me.

"I recently ended something, or I guess you can call it that," I said, frustrated. "And I'm not looking to meet anyone new right now."

I felt rather sorry for myself at that moment.

"But thank you anyway," I added.

"No one in their right mind would break up with you," he replied, chuckling.

I grinned when I noticed his beautiful blue eyes as he kept smiling at me.

"Has that line ever worked for you?" I asked. John laughed.

"Sometimes it does," he said with an inquisitive grin.

"Would you like to dance?" he asked in a much deeper voice,

speaking louder to carry over the music.

I don't know exactly what I was in the mood for, but I wanted to get out of my slump and stop feeling sorry for myself. I kept thinking, What if Mark showed up tomorrow? So what if he did? I have no commitment to him. He's the one who hasn't called me in a month, and he's married to a woman. I could have called him, but maybe I was giving him the space he needed to figure out his own life, or was I happy he was gone? And once again, I thought, Was he lying to me the whole time?

Dr. Smith's voice echoed in my mind. "*Mark is bad for you, and another big dick will not fill your loneliness.*" But I thought that a big dick did sound awfully good.

"So ... John ... is it?

"Yes. John Montgomery."

"What are you looking for, a fuck or a dance?" I stated sharply.

"Wow," John said, with a surprised look on his face. Then he laughed a little.

"I'm so tired of men not knowing how to express themselves and say what they want," I said boldly. "And I don't usually do one-night stands."

He chuckled.

If I were him, I'd be chuckling too because ninety-nine percent of the gay men I've met are liars if they say they don't do one-night stands. I've had many one-night stands in the twenty-five years I've been out of the closet. And I don't know why I lied to him. I think at that moment, I just wanted him to go away. But a microsecond later, I changed my mind. I'm a complex person.

"But from time to time they do pop into my life, so tonight I want to get fucked and fucked hard," I added.

John stood quietly in front of me, grinning from ear to ear as I continued.

"Do you have a big dick, John, because I love big dicks," I acknowledged melodramatically.

"I have an above-average-sized dick," John said. "It's only seven inches long, but it is thick."

"My dick is just average, John. Is that okay with you?" I thought my comment about having an average-sized dick would scare him away.

John lightly laughed at me as I made my ridiculous statements.

"That's fine," he said, smiling.

I looked at John, puzzled, wondering why the average-dick comment didn't chase him away as it does most gay men, even though they are tops. I guessed even tops want something fat to suck on. But did I want to chase him away? I didn't think so, because getting fucked was something I wanted. My toy wasn't going to do the trick.

"I don't want to get into a bad situation if I take you home with me, so could I take a picture of us and text it to my friend I am here with tonight?" I asked.

"No problem," he replied.

I texted my friend. *He's fucking me tonight.*

I saw my friend across the dance floor as he opened my text. I waved to him, and he gave me the thumbs-up with a big smile.

I asked John if he drove here.

"No," he replied.

"Where do you live?" I asked.

I didn't want to drive far to take him home later.

"I live in Glendale, about fifteen minutes away," John replied.

At least it wasn't a ninety-minute round trip, or he could

take a cab.

"Not to be too blunt, but if we are going to fuck, we have to go now, because I hate when guys wait until the bar closes and you're too tired at two in the morning to get a good fuck in," I stated.

"I agree with the two a.m. thing, but you're a little too late on the bluntness. You just asked me if I wanted a fuck or a dance, didn't you?" John replied, still smiling.

"Oh, yeah, I did, didn't I?" I chuckled.

Throughout our conversation, John maintained a smile on his face.

"I've got one last question before I go home with you," John asked.

"What's that?"

"What is your name?" John grinned at me.

"Oh my god ... I am so sorry. My name is Alex, Alex Morgan."

"It is nice to meet you, Alex, and I can't wait to fuck you." He chuckled.

I laughed, realizing how ridiculous I must have sounded spouting off with my demands or whatever they were.

It was only eleven o'clock when we got to my place. I asked him if he wanted anything to drink.

"Water is fine," he replied.

Now that we were in a well-lit room, I could see a decent bulge in his pants. I gave him his glass of water, and he took a small sip before setting it down on a coaster on the coffee table. To me, that showed respect for other people's property.

He grabbed the front of my shirt, gently pulling me toward him, and kissed me—first a quick peck, then a second kiss that lasted much longer. Slowly, he licked the outer rim of my lips. I moaned. He pressed his erection against mine through our jeans. He parted my lips with his tongue, giving himself full access to my mouth. I sucked on his tongue until he withdrew it.

"Oh my," I said breathlessly.

He pressed his erection against mine with more urgency.

"If we're going to be honest and direct about everything," he said matter-of-factly, "did you want to get right to the fucking, or did you want to do some exploring on each other first?"

Before I could answer, he continued. "And by the way, I always use condoms. If that's not okay, we are not fucking, but we can do everything else though."

"Yes, I always use condoms too," I replied hesitantly.

I didn't think I would see John again, so I didn't tell him about Mark.

"I'd like to do other things," I replied. John smiled.

John requested that we take a shower so we would be nice and clean for each other.

"I was going to suggest the same thing. No dirty bodies for me, please," I told him.

"Is there anything off-limits in our exploring?" John asked.

"I don't think so."

"I like my butt rimmed. Would that be okay? If so, I will make sure I am nice and clean for you," John added.

"With the right person, I love doing that, and I think I would like to do that with you, John," I told him with a grin on my face.

I removed his clothes one piece at a time. I have always enjoyed helping a good-looking man get undressed—one layer at a time, like unwrapping a present. John hadn't lost his smile since the moment I met him at the club. Removing a man's pants and watching his dick fall out for the first time is exciting.

I was not disappointed when I opened my present. As I pulled down his boxer briefs, his seven-inch, very thick dick fell out. I swear I almost drooled. Thickness has always been more important to me than length, and seven inches was perfect.

John returned the favor by helping me undress. After he removed each item of my clothing, he kissed me. I liked the way he undressed me. With every kiss, he made me smile. Usually, I take the initiative when it comes to kissing and touching, but tonight it was all John. I guess he could tell that I wasn't used to the attention. Every time I reached for him, he would grab my hands and ask me to be patient.

"We'll get there," he said. I smiled.

I didn't have to wait long for all his first moves; they were coming one after another, and I was enjoying them so much.

Throughout my life, I was always the one making the first move. Otherwise, there was no foreplay—just sex. Who knows why I do anything? My insecurities are inconsistent, so I never know why or what I will do in any situation. So when John wanted to take care of me, I didn't know how to react. It was totally foreign to me because it was something I had received very few times in my life.

I told John he could have some privacy in my bathroom while I went to the hallway bathroom and properly prepared myself for him.

"Thanks, I'll do the same," John replied.

"Open the door when you're done so I don't walk in if you are in the middle of something," I chuckled.

"I will," he added.

When I walked into my bathroom, John was standing in the shower with his back towards me, with the water running over him. He had a beautifully tanned body, except for where his

Speedo covered him. The water flowed over his head, down his back, and over his delicious-looking butt cheeks, where I knew I would be in just a short amount of time.

His butt made me take a deep breath as my heart beat a little faster. I had to keep reminding myself that this was only a one-night stand and not to get too attached. After joining him in the shower, he gave me another kiss before he soaped up a washcloth and started washing me. He took me by my shoulders and turned me around to face him. He smiled at me while I looked into his beautiful blue eyes. He gently grabbed my dick and kissed me. He pulled on my penis a couple more times before he continued washing me.

"Spread your legs so I can wash your undercarriage. I want every inch of you clean to explore later," John said seductively.

"Anything you say," I replied.

He rinsed my upper body with the handheld shower head before kneeling to wash my legs and feet. He put my dick into his mouth and held on tight with his lips as he began washing. Without letting me fall out of his mouth, he motioned with his hand for me to raise each foot one at a time so he could wash them. I balanced myself, holding his shoulders while he was doing this feat of magic. He was very entertaining. I caught myself crushing on him because he was being so attentive to me.

He told me to close my eyes so he could wash my face and ears. I liked it when he told me what to do, listening to his deep voice. But as I was enjoying John, I was also thinking about Mark and our first night together. They were one hundred percent different.

While my eyes were still closed, he rinsed me off from top to bottom.

"Can I do the same for you?" I asked.

"No, thank you. But I will tell you what you can do for me," he replied.

Excitement flowed through me.

"Dry yourself off, get into bed, gather everything we will need for later, and set it on the nightstand," he said while kissing my cheek and smiling.

"Then I want you to lie on your back playing with yourself, but don't use any lube," he said with a devilish grin. I snickered.

"While you are playing with yourself, I will finish my shower, making sure I am spotless for you. Then I will kiss you from your toes to your lips, to your nipples, to your dick," John said. I moaned.

"I will roll you over onto your stomach, lick your butt, and play with your dick until you beg me to let you come, but I will stop in time so you don't."

He kissed me on my lips softly. A hum escaped my throat.

"Then I will roll you onto your back, and it will be your turn to do the same to me. And when you're done doing me, I will fuck your brains out if that's what you still want," John added, gazing into my eyes.

I think my face was about to split in half from the massive smile on it. I had never had anyone explain in such detail what they were going to do to me. I could not wait to get started.

"Can you do me one favor before I start doing you?" I asked.

"What's that?"

"When you roll me onto my back, would you raise my legs and do my butt one more time before I start doing you. Getting rimmed with my legs over my head is my favorite position," I added.

John laughed.

"Of course I will ... you have a beautiful butt," John acknowledged.

I stood inside the shower listening to my instructions. I felt as if I could have had an orgasm just listening to him. Both of us were as hard as steel. His deep voice made me want to fall to the floor and let him do whatever he wanted to do to my body.

I got out of the shower and dried myself off. I followed his instructions and got everything needed for the evening's event: lube, condoms, towels, hand cloths, and extra sheets, just in case these sheets ended up with too much lube on them.

I pulled down the top sheet and blanket to the bottom of the bed. I added two more pillows at the head of the bed. I was lying on my back playing with myself. I didn't play too hard because I was so turned on that I could have shot at any moment. I watched him from my bed as he dried himself off. He was still semi-hard. He was not one of those gay guys who trimmed off all his body hair, but he did trim it down some, which I liked. I like hair just where it belongs. As he was drying off, he pulled on his dick to get fully erect as he looked at me lying on the bed. He was still smiling. I was starting to get attached to his smile.

His smile grew bigger as he entered my bedroom. He stood at the end of the bed and said that he loved to watch a handsome man jerking off.

"Even my little dick?" I responded.

"You have an average-sized dick. I've seen smaller dicks in the locker room at the gym. Yours has to be six inches because it touched the back of my throat in the shower. Your dick is perfect for me. So do not put yourself down like that again, please?" he said with a big smile as he leaned down to kiss me.

I smiled back at him, but I was about to cry. He said my dick was perfect for him. No one has ever told me I was perfect for them in any way before.

He stood at the end of the bed, playing with himself as he watched me. I loved looking at this six-foot-tall man with light brown hair, blue eyes, and a well-toned body staring down at me. I prefer a well-toned body over an overly developed muscular one any day of the week.

He did exactly what he said he would do. He slowly moved from my feet upward, stopped to kiss my penis before moving up my chest to my lips. He nibbled on my earlobes, kissed my neck, then my nose, and then my mouth. He had great lips; I didn't want to let them go. He kissed me from my head to my toes and back up again. He rolled me over onto my stomach. The things his tongue did to my hole were amazing. He sucked my dick until I begged him to let me come. He did as he promised and didn't let me.

"It's your turn to do me," John stated, deepening his voice.

"Do me one more time?" I reminded him.

He turned me over, raised my legs; he devoured my butt like no one ever had before. I moaned, I squirmed, I wanted to get fucked at that very moment, but I hadn't fulfilled my part of our agreement yet. So I had to wait for my turn. I swear he could teach a college course on oral sex.

He had no problem telling me if I was doing something he didn't like or if I was stopping too soon, but he did so very gently. I didn't mind receiving instructions because I want to make my sex partner happy. When my tongue reached his backside, he must have agreed that I knew what I was doing, because the more my tongue went in, the more, oh my god, escaped his throat. I loved that he kept pushing his butt tighter against my face as my tongue went deeper into him.

It's a good thing we started earlier in the evening, because it was nearing one thirty a.m. When his turn came again, John climbed between my legs as he reached for a condom, lube, and a cloth from the nightstand as we both nearly toppled off the bed onto the floor. He stopped us from falling by placing his right hand on the corner of the nightstand. We both laughed.

"Before we start, do you still want to get fucked hard from the very start, or did you want something else by now? I don't mind plowing you if that is what you want," he said mischievously.

I swear I heard a little Southern drawl when he said, "Or did you want something else by now?" Oh boy, a Texan, I thought.

"Are you from Texas?" I asked.

"Yes," he replied. "My dad was transferred for work to Los Angeles when I was fourteen."

He smiled and kissed me again; I returned the kiss.

"Does my being from Texas excite you?" John asked.

I didn't say anything. I just nodded to acknowledge yes.

John chuckled.

"Well, I do have a cowboy hat and boots. I wear them when I go to the rodeo and country western dancing," John stated in a sexy tone, trying to bring out more of his accent.

I wished that this wasn't just a one-night stand because my fantasies were running wild. John in a cowboy hat, oh my.

"Can we start with something slower at first? Everything we've been doing so far has put me in a different state of mind than I was earlier. But later on, we can build up the intensity, especially at the end," I replied.

"Your wish is my command, sir," John said, smiling.

He aligned himself with my hole and gently pushed inward. As soon as he was inside me, my legs immediately wrapped around his waist and pulled him into me. He filled me so wonderfully. I opened my mouth wide and took in a deep breath.

A large smile appeared on my face. John smiled back. He started by moving gently inside me and kept building the intensity as I moaned louder with his inward thrust. I kept squeezing my butt muscles tighter as he moved inside me. John must have liked the squeezing because he moved faster when I did. I didn't mean to, but I kept thinking of Mark while John was fucking me. Each time, I pushed those thoughts out of my mind quickly. I made sure not to talk. I did not want to call John the wrong name. Even though my mind was having flashbacks of Mark, I knew that it was John deep inside me, and I was thrilled that he was.

I didn't realize how long he had been inside me. John fucked me in at least five positions. I turned my head towards the clock on my nightstand and saw that fifty-five minutes had passed by. I was thoroughly enjoying our time together. He was making love to me, not just having sex. He was so playful that he made me laugh; he told bad jokes, and I laughed at them anyway. He kissed me hard and then pushed his tongue deep into my mouth. I loved sucking on his tongue. This made me so hot that I started to pulse my lower body hard against him to push his dick deeper inside me if that was at all possible.

He arched his body over mine and gave me a devilish look.

"Is this what you were asking for at the club?" he asked, as he started fucking me hard for several minutes with a large smile on his face. Ramming his penis deeper inside me until his body was tight against mine. I didn't say a word back to him. I grabbed my ankles and pulled them back as far as I could, giving him a better aim at my bottom. His smile got bigger the harder he rammed me.

I could feel my insecurities surfacing as tears started to form in my eyes.

"Are you okay?" John asked.

I pushed back the tears as hard as I could.

"I'm fine. I'm having such a great time, and sometimes I get emotional," I told him. "Please don't stop."

John did as I asked. I guided my mind back to the feeling of John moving in and out of me. I love that sensation. I needed him inside me. Getting fucked is how I cope with unhealthy relationships. But would John be in an unhealthy relationship? I pulled his lips toward mine and kissed him hard.

I couldn't hold back any longer; I needed John to fuck me harder because I needed to have an orgasm. I squeezed my butt muscles as tight as I could; this made John move faster, and I held them tight until I came. John wasn't far behind me with his release. I told him to keep going until he was done, which was about a minute away. I held my muscles tight as he came inside me. I imagined him filling me up with his warm liquids, but in reality, he was filling a condom.

He was still inside me as we kept kissing. My legs remained wrapped around his waist. I didn't want to let him go. His beautiful blue eyes looked into mine. I could feel tears welling up again as he gently pulled himself out of me. I managed to hold them back once more as my insecurities reared their ugly head. Regardless of whether my emotions were good or bad, they always showed in my eyes. Why couldn't I have a panic attack like most sane people instead of crying? John saw what was happening again, but he said nothing; he just kissed me again and smiled.

I hadn't planned for John to spend the night, but it was late, and I wasn't getting out of bed. Plus, after he pulled himself out of me, he wrapped his body around my backside and hugged me tight. I melted into him. He kissed the back of my neck. I softly moaned each time he did. He pressed his dick against my butt crack as he squeezed me one more time.

"Are you okay with spending the night?" I asked him. "I'm too tired to drive."

"I don't want to get out of bed either. I'm very happy where I am," he uttered softly.

He kissed me one more time. Within minutes, we started falling asleep. We didn't care that we were sticky; we were simply tired.

Plus, I didn't want him to let me go.

8

Chapter Eight

I was lying on my side, facing away from John, when I woke. I rolled over to look at him, and the condom was the first thing I saw. He had no sheet over him. I started laughing, and my laughter was what woke him.

"Why are you laughing?" John asked, with his eyes barely open.

"Look at your dick," I replied, chuckling.

His eyes widened; he had forgotten to take off the condom. He burst out laughing.

"I must have been so tired I didn't feel it on me," John said.

We both laughed.

He leaned in to kiss me and said, "Good morning. I had such a good time last night."

"So did I," I replied, smiling.

It was nearing ten a.m. when John looked at the clock.

"I made plans for Sunday brunch with friends at eleven a.m.," he said excitedly.

"I won't have enough time to go home, shower, dress, and drive to West Hollywood. Would you like to go to breakfast with me and meet my friends I was with last night?"

I paused while taking a deep breath, thinking about how I should answer.

"It's not a good idea," I said while shaking my head. "But you can take a shower here and borrow some of my clothes. I think we are about the same size, and I can drop you off at the restaurant. And I have a new toothbrush you can have."

"Why don't you want to go?" he asked.

"I'm not a fan of the morning-after fuck jokes," I replied hesitantly.

I wasn't sure whether that was the real reason I didn't want to go, or I was just afraid of getting hurt again. And what if John's friends were like mine and made fun of me? John is a nice guy. But when anyone turns out to be as wonderful as he was, they usually end up hurting me in the end. And I'm just so tired of being hurt. Still, Dr. Smith and I had been discussing the possibility of introducing a nice guy into my life while keeping an eye out for potential red flags. I would see her on Tuesday evening and could discuss John with her then.

"Well, I can't promise there won't be any morning-after fuck jokes, but I'd really like to see you a little longer if I could," he said with a grin.

"No, this was just a one-night stand," I said matter-of-factly.

"Does it have to be? Please come," John replied with hope in his eyes.

I thought about it for a few minutes and realized I also wanted to spend a little more time with John. We woke up laughing this morning, and it had been so long since I woke up laughing with someone.

"Well, call and tell your friends that we'll be just a little late. Let's jump into the shower and get moving," I muttered with a bit of hesitation in my voice and a little bit of excitement. John smiled and clapped his hands.

This time, due to our time constraints, we washed ourselves in the shower. But John did take a moment to wash my undercarriage.

"Look through my dresser for underwear, socks, or whatever you need, John," I said.

It felt as if we had done this many times before. We were so in sync. I felt relaxed around John. He made me feel wanted. It wasn't like most one-night stands, where the guy was up and out the door as soon as his eyes opened.

As John opened one of my dresser drawers, he smiled widely and pulled out my large dildo. I had moved it from my bathroom closet so no one could accidentally find it again.

John held it into the air, still smiling, and said, "I hope I get to use this on you sometime. I want to see the expression on your face when I shove it into your butt."

"Oh my god," I stated with my hand over my mouth. "I forgot it was in that drawer."

I took it from him, placed it back into the drawer, and covered it with my clean underwear.

"I guess you weren't kidding when you said you like big dicks. I hope I was enough for you last night," he said, smiling.

"Yes, John, you were more than enough for me last night," I said, a little embarrassed.

He giggled.

One time, my out-of-town house guests, two old college

friends who visit every summer, were here for a weekend. They needed towels to take to the pool at my condo.

"Where are the towels?" Kyle had asked.

They're in my bathroom closet," I said.

Before I could say another word, I heard a thud on the tile floor, and Kyle screeched out, "Oh my god!" They shriek about everything because they are the two biggest queens I know. I ran to the bathroom as Kyle held up my large dildo in one hand. He raised it high above his head like a trophy, with the biggest smirk on his face. I thought it was hidden well enough so no one could find it. When he'd grabbed a couple of towels from the shelf, my toy fell onto the floor. He was laughing so hard that tears ran down his cheeks.

His boyfriend, Ray, rushed in because he thought one of us had fallen. When Ray saw what was happening, he shouted in a high-pitched voice, "Oh my god, you really do like big dicks, don't you?" I turned bright red. As Kyle kept holding it up, he proclaimed, "I dub you, Sir Herk." We all bowed to Sir Herk. We looked at one another for a moment of silence. Then, we burst into laughter.

"We need to get our act together so we're not too late for brunch," I said.

"Yes, sir, boss man," John said, chuckling.

John leaned in and kissed me.

I guided him to the closet where I kept my shirts and pants. John was a picky dresser, so he changed clothes three times.

I was a little larger built than he was, but not by much. By the time he got my clothes to fit with rolled-up sleeves and rolled-up pant cuffs, he looked like he was living in the 1950s.

"You won't look out of place," I said. "Everyone in West Hollywood has their own style."

John viewed himself in my full-length mirror on my closet door.

"Well, if anyone is going to get the after-morning fuck jokes, it will be me. I'm wearing your clothes that don't fit." John chuckled.

"But you look gorgeous in my clothes, John," I said as I looked at this handsome man.

"You think I am gorgeous," he replied caringly.

"Yes, I do," I said softly as I gazed into his blue eyes.

John leaned in and kissed me, a long, slow kiss that made me want to pull him back into bed. I appreciate that John doesn't hold back his emotions.

"Okay, let's get going," I commanded. "I hate being late."

"Yes, sir," he replied as he held me tight one more time and dug his tongue deep into my mouth. I could get so used to this, I thought as I attempted to catch my breath.

We were the last to arrive at the restaurant, but only twenty minutes late. Luckily, there wasn't much traffic, or we would have been much later.

"I love The French Market, and especially their bran muffins," I said.

I was glad we were inside and not outside on the front patio, because on a Sunday morning, traffic on Santa Monica Boulevard is noisy.

As we walked closer to the table, everyone started to laugh. I was preparing myself for the morning-after fuck jokes.

"Where did you get those clothes, John? Is this what you call 'walk of shame' fashion? Did you lose weight?" asked a man with blond hair.

"Ok, guys, that's enough," John said sternly.

"I don't think so, John. We've just gotten started," said

another man with light brown hair, jokingly.

"You don't usually go home with anyone. So this is a new look for you," said another man at the table, chuckling as he looked at John.

"Before you all continue making fun of me, you jerks, I'd like to introduce my friends to you, Alex," John said.

I smiled nervously as everyone laughed.

"Everyone, this is Alex. Alex, this is Paul and Bob. They have been together for ten years. These guys who have been making the most fun of me are Harry and Ben. They have been together for what, seven years now? And these two quiet people are Carlos and Mike. They are the newest members of the married crowd," John acknowledged with a big smile. "And, believe it or not, they are all my best friends."

"And John's been divorced for two years now. Did he tell you that, Alex? And we are all trying to find him a husband, just in case you are interested," said Ben, the man with the light brown hair.

"But John does come with baggage. He has four kids and an ex-wife, and they are all fantastic people," Ben continued.

"Ben, you can shut up now," John requested.

I just stood there smiling, unsure of what to say. But I could tell from their joshing that these friends cared about each other. I usually feel anxious when meeting new people, but they instantly made me feel like part of the group by including me in the conversation.

John did everything he could to keep the morning-after fuck jokes away from me. But I shouldn't have worried because the guys were having too much fun focusing all their attention on John. There was no harshness behind their comments, just a lot of friendly banter and love. John laughed along with them, not to appease them as I would have, but because he knew his friends meant no harm, I believed. John was someone I wished I could be—a strong, confident person who loved himself, based on what I have seen of him so far. These are the type of friends I'd been searching for my whole life, and I hoped I'd get the chance to get to know them better.

"How late did you guys stay at the club after I left?" John asked his friends.

"We stayed till midnight ... old folks, you know," Ben replied.

"We don't go out that often, unless it's to a concert, a play, or dinner and a movie, Alex. We'd rather spend time together at one of our houses. We just wanted to get John out of the house on a Saturday night. We weren't expecting him to go home with someone," Harry exclaimed. They all smiled.

They discussed their plans for summer vacation. They all planned to go to Provincetown in early September when the weather cooled down. Otherwise, it was just too humid to enjoy themselves.

"And we're also going to Hawaii in late October. We have more fun if we go in a group," Harry told me excitedly.

"I've worked with John for many years and had always thought that he was a good guy. So, when he got divorced and told me he was gay, we all took him under our wing. We are his gay parents, and we will not let anyone hurt him," Harry continued.

John placed his hand on top of mine. I chuckled instead of letting my eyes well up. I felt relaxed with John next to me. He seemed to sense when I felt nervous.

"Harry, you can stop singing my praises now," John uttered.

"I don't think he'll stop until he finds you a husband," Ben chuckled, and I laughed.

"Knowing John as I do, I didn't believe he was the promiscuous type or someone who partied a lot. He had a family and was mainly just a straight guy. Our group has just added a little more spice to his life, but not too much spice," Harry said. We all chuckled.

***

After finishing our meals, we said goodbye and left our table. I got hugs from everyone. It took several minutes for everyone to say goodbye, as they all had to hug each other. It was a funny sight to watch, but also made me want to cry. These people cared about each other, not like my friends who came to dinner on my birthday.

After brunch, I drove John home. He asked if he could put his hand on my knee as we drove past the Hollywood Bowl. I told him it was okay. I was surprised when he asked because, in my experience, most gay men don't ask; they take what they want. We didn't talk much on the way to his house, or I didn't speak much to him. The traffic was heavy, and I prefer to focus on my driving when it's congested. I think John sensed my nervousness, just as he had at the restaurant, as my hands were tightly gripping the steering wheel.

John lived two blocks from his children and ex-wife on the same street.

"Would you like to come in so we can visit a little longer?" John asked.

I couldn't believe the size of John's house. It looked like a mansion to me—a two-story red brick Georgian-style. It was beautiful. Most of the neighborhood was characterized by a similar style. What did he do for a living to have such a home? How much money did he make? My insecurities were taking charge. I already knew I wasn't good enough for him. But I remembered what Dr. Smith had been trying her best to teach me. I'm a good person, and someone will see that. So I took a deep breath.

"Sure," I replied hesitantly.

As soon as we got into his house, John pulled me in close and gave me a gentle kiss. He smiled. I could feel the tears coming into my eyes again, but I did everything I could to hold them back.

"Things make you emotional, don't they?" he asked caringly.

I took a deeper breath.

"Yes, yes, they do," I replied nervously.

He kissed me, but didn't say anything.

The horrible thoughts running through my mind stemmed from all the terrible boyfriends I'd had over the years. The relationship started out great—like a dream come true; they were attentive, loving, romantic—everything someone could wish for. They said they loved me and I was the person they had been searching for. Then, out of nowhere, they began treating me like trash. I couldn't do anything right; I'm too moody; I'm too needy. Before long, they would break up with me. I'd be heartbroken once again. Now, I was afraid that John would do the same thing.

The reason I wanted to cry was that I could feel the pain coming my way. But this time, like all the others, I hoped I was wrong. Or maybe the others were never attentive. Perhaps they always treated me like garbage. And maybe I was just pretending they cared so I didn't have to face the truth about being the dysfunctional person I am and that I am unlovable.

John looked at me with those beautiful blue eyes, which made me melt the more I saw them. I wanted to believe that this time would turn out better.

"Can I see you again?" he asked softly.

" I guess if I want my clothes back, I have to see you again," I replied jokingly.

John laughed and gave me another kiss.

"I need to tell you something about myself before you make a final decision on seeing me again," I said hesitantly.

"You can tell me anything," he added.

I took a deep breath.

"I'm not a promiscuous man. But sometimes I am, because otherwise I get lonely. I don't go to bars a lot to pick up guys, but I love to dance, and the young guys pay a lot of attention to me when I take my shirt off." I'm talking nervously as John listens.

"I want to build a life with someone, hopefully, before it's too late. I am fifty years old, and I haven't found it yet. Sometimes I'm a complete emotional mess, and I scare people away." I kept rambling.

Tears were slowly running down my cheeks. I couldn't hold them back.

"I believe I have never dated anyone who hasn't cheated on me, even though I thought we were in a monogamous relationship. When I asked why they lied, one man told me that gay men don't live in monogamy, and he told me what he thought I wanted to hear," I added.

John sat in the chair across from me, listening intently without interrupting.

"I think we are a lot alike, from what I got from your friends today. The person you met in the bar last night was not the real me. But because of things that have happened to me over the years and the household I was raised in, I am a very insecure person. I get a little too needy sometimes, and it becomes more than some can handle. You saw just a little bit of it last night when you asked me if something was wrong, and you're seeing it right now with the tears running down my face. I don't mean to be so needy, but like I said, I have never found someone who didn't cheat on me, and that is all I have ever wanted, and I don't think it is too much to ask of someone," I continued, still rambling and maybe not making a lot of sense.

I'm glad he didn't say anything, because I would have lost my train of thought.

"Plus, I still think of that guy who dumped me. It was a bad situation to begin with. He was just coming out, or I thought he was, unless he lied to me. And he wasn't divorced yet. He just disappeared, no goodbye, nothing, just gone. We didn't know each other for very long, but I fell hard for him, or maybe I fell hard just because I am so tired of being by myself. I don't know how long it will take to get him out of my system, but I do know that if he called me today, I would tell him to go away."

"Would you?" John asked pensively.

"Yes, I would, John. I honestly would," I replied.

John pressed his lips together and nodded like he believed me.

"So, knowing this stuff about me, if you would like to go out again, I would very much like to," I stated breathlessly.

"Go out again?" John asked.

"I'm sorry. Wasn't brunch a date?" I said in a panicked tone.

"Yes, it was a date. For me, anyway. I'm glad you thought it was a date." John chuckled.

I exhaled a deep breath to relax.

"Oh, one more thing about me, John. Well, two more things. First, by the looks of this house, I can't afford the things you can, so dinners and things have to be on the inexpensive side.

And second, when I get insecure, I ask for a lot of sex. It's my coping mechanism," I said, grinning.

John giggled.

"Well, Alex. First, I can handle all the sex you may need, and second, inexpensive is fine," John stated, grinning.

"I would like to spend time getting to know you, Alex. We can get to know each other gradually. But let me give you the basics about my family and me," he said caringly.

"My family is the most important thing in my life. Sometimes my children will have to come first. However, as we get to know each other, you will be invited to join our activities. I am still very close to my ex-wife, but there will never be a reason for you to get jealous of her. Toward the end of our marriage, she was having a hard time with me pulling away from her, as my attraction toward men was growing stronger. After I told her I thought I was gay, it was a relief to her because she was taking all the blame upon herself. I didn't want to hurt her anymore because I did love her. She is my best friend," John continued.

I started to cry again as John walked over to the sofa and sat next to me. He kissed my cheek.

"Alison and I sat down one night to tell the children that we were getting a divorce and why. We wanted to make sure that the kids knew we both loved them and would always be there for them. The kids adapted to me being two blocks away quite easily because they knew I would always be nearby. They have two homes now. And they each have their own bedrooms at my house, just like they do at the house they were raised in," John acknowledged.

"We have two boys and two girls, ranging in age from seven to twenty. They spend a lot of time at my house. We don't follow a fixed schedule where they are with me one week and with their mom the next. They needed to keep the same routine they were used to. I see them every day, even if it's just for a few minutes. They call me whenever they need me. I can't go a day without seeing them. At first, it was hard for me when they weren't at my house in the evenings at bedtime. I missed them so much. I was lonely, and I cried myself to sleep every night for several weeks until I got used to the house feeling empty. I have never told anyone this before— not even my closest friends, not even Alison—and I can't believe I'm telling you," John said sadly.

John and I faced each other, sitting sideways on the couch as he talked. I was still crying a little, and so was he. He was a pillar of strength until he mentioned his kids. I pulled him closer and wrapped my arms around him. He kissed me.

"It's getting harder to see the oldest two kids every day because they are so busy with school and dating, but we make it work. I have found that the typical gay man finds dealing with school activities too constraining for them and doesn't like playing second fiddle to my kids. I am also looking for the same type of relationship you are looking for. I guarantee that I am not lying to you. If we are still seeing each other in a few months, and I hope we are, I will not start mistreating you and break up with you. Just tell me when you are feeling insecure, and we can talk it through just like I do with my ex-wife and kids. We are not a perfect family, and we can create our share of drama. Plus, I only want to share myself and my body with one other person," John said caringly.

John pulled me in close to him and kissed me. I was already getting used to his kisses.

"I can't see you again until next weekend because my schedule is already filled with activities for the kids all week. They have numerous school functions," John said. I frowned.

"So, could I see you for dinner later tonight? I'll pick you up at seven at your condo," John added.

"Why can't I pick you up and go to dinner in your neighborhood? Glendale has so many great restaurants," I asked.

"Well, I never know when one of the kids is going to pop in, and Bobby, the seven-year-old, is my most frequent visitor. And to put it bluntly. I would like to fuck you again tonight if that's okay," John said with a smile that made my heart beat faster.

"Is that all you want me for, a fuck?" I asked, worried.

"You didn't listen to me, did you?" John said. "I want to get to know you. I had such a great time last night, I don't want to wait a whole week before I get to do it again. So let me put it this way. Can I make love to you again tonight, please?" John asked, caringly.

I took a deep breath.

"Pick me up at seven, please," I replied, wide-eyed.

9

Chapter Nine

John kept his promise. Every time my insecurities surfaced, and I shared them with him, he was there to support me. We talked about everything from our childhoods to the present day. John's childhood, like everyone's, had its rough patches, but mostly it was filled with loving, supportive parents. My parents argued constantly, mainly because of my mother. She was a very angry woman who hated everything around her, especially me. I was her favorite punching bag.

My father was never involved in my life. He ignored me as if I didn't exist. But when he did talk to me, it wasn't always pleasant.

"I made one mistake in life, and that was having you as a son," he would say.

So every time I make a mistake, even today, I still hear those words crashing down on me. They hurt just as much now as they did when I was a child.

I was shocked by the nonsense John was willing to tolerate during our first two weeks of dating. I acted like a child, throwing multiple temper tantrums. He set clear boundaries by the end of the second week, stating that this kind of behavior was unacceptable around his family, especially his children. During one appointment with Dr. Smith, she called me out for my childish behavior.

"Why are you working so hard to wreck things with John?" she asked pointedly.

"Because I'm no good, and I have to chase him away before he hurts me," I replied.

"You have a handsome man sitting in the waiting room, wanting to help you get through your struggles so you can have a better life. You didn't ask him to come. He came on his own. And he doesn't need another child in his life. He already has four. What he needs is a partner—someone to love, care for, make love to, and share his life with. So get your act together," she said matter-of-factly.

I was crying so hard that John heard me from the waiting room. John knocked softly on the door.

"Can I come in?" he asked.

Dr. Smith got up from her chair to open the door, which was locked from the inside.

"Come in, John," she said.

John sat down next to me, and I immediately wrapped my arms around him and cried. Dr. Smith watched our interaction before she spoke.

"John," she said firmly.

John tilted his head upward from my shoulder to look at her.

"You can't be a crutch for Alex. You can be someone he leans on from time to time until he finds his footing, but if you keep being his crutch, he'll never develop new life patterns," she said supportively.

John released his tight hold on me, but he didn't let go of me completely. I released a deep breath.

"I have been trying to teach this old dog new tricks for the past two years," she said, smiling.

John had a shocked look on his face from her comment.

"I like it when she talks like that," I said, chuckling. John kissed my cheek.

"He fights me tooth and nail because he is convinced he is a worthless human being, but John, I can see in your eyes that you don't believe that about him. You see the person I see. He's just too scared to trust, even though he wants to so badly. So, with your help, John, perhaps together we can help this guy love himself. How about it, boys, together?" she asked caringly. "You're a strong man, John, and I need your help because I know Alex is worth the effort."

John looked at me, I looked at him, and then we both looked at Dr. Smith and chuckled.

"Isn't she great?" I told John.

"I see why you like her so much," John replied.

***

John and I passed the three-month mark, and that's when most of the men have ended things with me. I sometimes wondered whether there was a set of rules that gay men follow that I didn't know about, because it seemed as if many men I've dated stick to the three-month rule.

The more time I spent with John, the more he taught me about the importance of honest and effective communication. This is something he had with his family, kids, and ex-wife. It wasn't a trait I learned within the family that raised me. We were dysfunctional, with no trust.

John could tell when something was bothering me, so when I wouldn't open up about it, he knew how to gently coax it out of me without being mean. When I first met John, I told him how I used sex as my coping mechanism. So after one of our talks, he asked, "Can I make love to you now?"

"Yes, please," I answered.

I pressed my face into his chest for comfort. In many ways, I was quite immature for a fifty-year-old man. But this didn't bother John. He made me feel safe and protected. He was the man I had been searching for my entire life. John didn't see me as a burden. By continuing to work with Dr. Smith during my first month of dating John, I wasn't throwing temper tantrums anymore, but my anxiety was still there.

I was in love with John, but I was too afraid to be the first to say those words. I was getting to know his family, and they were getting to know me as well. Since John got divorced, he had never dated anyone for an extended period or included them in family events. However, his family could see that our relationship was different from his past ones. By our third week of dating, John invited me to nearly every event involving family or school functions for the kids. As time went on, instead of John inviting me, the kids or his ex-wife would ask me before John even had a chance.

Bobby, the youngest boy in the family, and I quickly formed a strong bond. He was just a smaller version of John, with similar looks and personality. The older three kids—one boy and two girls—resembled their mother more. Bobby is such a wonderful kid. In many ways, I was just a big kid myself, which might be why we got along so well. We talked about everything—from the kids at school to his best friend, sports, and girls. Even at seven years old, he had already started noticing girls, but he said they were confusing and he didn't understand why he was attracted to them. I giggled and told him he would understand more as he got older.

"They change their minds about things so quickly," he said thoughtfully.

I had to laugh.

"Yes, they do. And they've been doing that since I was your age. So I don't think they are going to change. We'll have to get used to it, I guess," I replied.

"I guess we will, Alex," Bobby answered. I laughed once more.

Whenever there were family gatherings, Bobby always came and sat next to me because he said he noticed how nervous I was around people I didn't know very well. He was becoming my little buddy. He knew that I was a very emotional person, and some things made me very nervous. His dad tried to explain my insecurity issues to him, but he was having a hard time understanding them. After just a short time of getting to know me, he ran and hugged me as soon as he saw me. I loved that he was always so happy to see me. I always wanted kids, but I thought it would never be in the cards for me.

"Why do you look so scared sometimes?" Bobby asked.

"Well, it's because of things that have happened to me in my past, from my childhood up to now. All those things have made me feel insecure and scared, and those emotions make me want to cry for almost no reason at all, and I have a hard time holding back my tears," I said while letting out a deep sigh.

"Dad said it's okay for boys to cry. So why do you have to hold in your tears?" Bobby asked.

"My dad taught me that it wasn't okay for a boy to cry, so I try to hold them inside. I think that makes me cry even more," I explained to Bobby.

"I like what my dad taught me better," Bobby said.

"Me too," I replied.

"I have a friend at school who cries a lot because some of the older boys pick on him because he doesn't like to fight, and they call him a sissy. I think he might be gay because he likes to hug me a lot," Bobby stated.

"Does that bother you when he hugs you?" I asked.

"No, it doesn't bother me. He's a nice kid. He has the best train set ever. And I would rather be hugged than get hit," Bobby answered.

"Does anyone pick on you at school or anywhere else?" I asked.

"No, because Sam taught me how to fight back," Bobby replied. Sam is the oldest of John's four children.

"Even though I might not win the fight every time," Bobby said gently, "Sam said, to never back down. When others see that I am not afraid, they will stop picking fights with me, and Sam was right. But I still wish they wouldn't pick on my friend. He doesn't like to fight. I want to step in and fight the mean kids for him, but as Sam taught me, he needs to learn how to defend himself, or people are going to pick on him forever."

I felt silly listening to a seven-year-old boy teach me, as an adult, something I wish I had learned when I was seven. But I had a father who didn't teach me anything because he didn't care about me.

When John and I crawled into bed that night, I told him about my talk with Bobby and the lesson I learned from a seven-year-old.

"It's never too late to learn a new lesson, no matter your age or who you learn from. You didn't have guidance as a kid, just bullies," John said softly as he held me close. My eyes filled with tears.

John never made a big deal about my tears; they were just part of me, and he accepted that fact.

"So don't feel foolish learning from a seven-year-old. That seven-year-old has a lot of support in his life from me, his mom, his two sisters—even though they fight all the time—and his older brother. He idolizes Sam. Take this as another learning moment. I learn from the kids all the time. They teach me about what their daily lives are like—things their mom and I don't experience anymore, like when we were their age. So, soak up the knowledge, young man," John said caringly as he hugged me tighter. "Now, young man, can I make love to you?"

"Yes, please," I replied, smiling.

John and I, after six months together, got our first HIV test. We took a second test a month later to make sure the first one wasn't a false negative. John has practiced safe sex ever since his divorce. I had to be honest with John and tell him about sex with Mark.

"I don't know why I didn't use condoms with Mark. I felt safe with him because he was in a relationship with a woman and said I was the first man he had ever had sex with or cheated on his wife," I said, feeling completely ashamed of myself.

"I could have just been stupid that night because of the pot. But I don't think so. Pot has never made me have unsafe sex with anyone else. Dr. Smith told me that both Mark and I were at an all-time low on our birthdays, feeling worthless, and maybe we didn't care enough that night to be safe," I said.

John knew Mark's first name, but I never told him his last

name, just in case he might know him by chance.

Our first and second tests came back negative. We discussed all our sexual partners from the past two years with the doctor. He told us that if we were in a committed, monogamous relationship, we were now free to do as we pleased. In the seven months John and I had been together, I was usually the bottom participant. I loved being on the bottom. John wasn't a fan of it, but he had tried it a couple of times with me. He said it was uncomfortable. I loved feeling John inside me without a condom that night.

"You feel so warm," John said, giggling as he slid inside me.

"I love you," he whispered in my ear as he slid in and out of me, making me moan.

I started to cry as I held him tightly with my arms. He stopped moving. I wrapped my legs around him so he couldn't get out.

"Why are you crying?" John asked caringly.

"Why do you think, you dope?" I blurted. John chuckled.

"You love me?" I asked.

"Yes, I love you," John said as he kissed me.

"Talk to me. Tell me how you're feeling," John asked softly as he stayed inside me, my legs wrapped around him.

"Whenever anyone has said those words, that's when things go wrong. I am afraid you will lose interest in me, and I don't want to lose you because I love you too," I said nervously.

John kissed my lips softly as he looked into my eyes.

"You won't lose me if you don't sabotage things. And even then, I'm not letting you go. Promise me that you'll continue talking to me about every little insecurity that comes into your sweet, thick head," John said so caringly.

"I promise," I stated, teary-eyed.

John kissed me so gently.

"Now, can I continue to fuck you, sir?" John asked.

"Yes, please," I replied.

My insecurities ran wild for the next two weeks. I kept thinking that John was going to break up with me. I was fortunate that he is a strong person. He was helping me overcome all my insecurities. And mine were endless. I asked John for a lot of sex, sometimes twice a day. I hadn't quite stopped using sex as my coping mechanism just yet, but I was working on it with Dr. Smith. I don't think he minded, especially since we didn't have to wear condoms. He hated wearing a condom, and I hated them inside of me. They irritated my bottom.

I was so afraid of being someone who John could not handle. However, I was doing significantly better than I was more than seven months ago. I have driven many men away over the years because of my insecurities. I'd panic if John's phone went to voice mail and I didn't know where he was or whom he was with. Because of my past experiences with others, my mind immediately jumped to the thought that he was with someone else. But I knew he was not.

When he called me back, which was almost immediately every time, I would sometimes be crying.

"Hi, sweetheart, you okay?" he said, answering his phone.

"No," I cried out.

John always let me know that he was telling the truth about where he was by having people around him say hello to me. He never told them the state I was in. That information stayed between John and me.

"I'm so sorry, John," I said.

"Don't apologize, sweetheart. I am always here for you. We'll get through this," John said caringly.

This time when he called, I could hear Bobby in the car with him.

"Hi Alex," Bobby yelled excitedly.

"Hi Bobby," I replied.

"I'm pulling up in front of Bobby's to drop him off. I'm going inside to talk with Alison about some upcoming events at school, and then I'm going home," John said.

"Are you going to be okay, or do you want to come over?"

"I want to come over," I replied, crying more softly now.

"I want to see Alex," Bobby shouted.

"Not tonight," John said. "Alex and I need to talk about something."

"What stuff?" Bobby asked.

"Adult stuff," John replied.

"Oh, shucks," Bobby stated.

After seven months together, I was basically living full-time at John's house. It was more practical because of the kids and all their activities. I mainly saw the three older kids at family events or school functions. Still, we had a weekly dinner at either John's or Alison's house, with all the kids there. I loved having them in my life. Since Bobby was young, he enjoyed going everywhere with John and me.

Even though we were now mostly living together, we still made sure we had plenty of date nights. We loved having Bobby with us. He didn't interfere with our romantic time or with John and me growing closer to each other. Plus, Alison had just started dating a man named Dave. He was a nice guy, but quiet. With Bobby spending more time with us, Alison had more alone time with Dave.

Dave had never been married and didn't have any kids. Bobby was a typical seven-year-old with a great deal of energy and a strong attention-seeking streak. I didn't think that Dave and Alison would be able to create a closeness between them if Bobby were always around on their dates or sleepovers at Alison's house. With Bobby spending more time with John and me, I feel even closer to John.

"Are you being romantic?" Bobby asked when he saw his dad kiss me in front of him.

John was honest with his kids, family, and friends about who he was. He was a confident man and wasn't ashamed of himself, even though he kept it hidden for half his life. If people didn't like who he was, he said that was their problem, not his.

"Yes, Bobby, we are being romantic," John replied. We all smiled.

The time was approaching when John and his friends planned a week in Provincetown. The trip was three weeks away, and John hadn't mentioned that I was going with him. My insecurities about John going to a town full of hot guys without me were making me crazy. I was trying my best not to show that it upset me. I should have talked to John before then.

We met the guys for dinner because we hadn't seen them in a couple of weeks. Work schedules and kids' functions kept us busy. The subject of Provincetown was brought up almost immediately.

"Has everyone put in for their vacation time?" Ben asked.

"Yes," everyone replied except me.

I could feel my eyes well up, and I tried to hold them back. Everyone could see what was happening to me; they knew about my insecurity issues. I had become emotional in front of them many times. They were always supportive as our friendships grew. They didn't make fun of me like others have in my past. Many times, they pulled me in for a group hug and made me laugh.

Ben looked at John and said, "Will you please stop it and ask him already?"

I hated feeling like a little kid sitting at the table, but this was how my insecurities worked.

John looked at me, smiled, and said, "Would you like to go with us? I don't think I could go an entire week without sleeping with you."

I looked at John and said, "I hate you."

"No, you don't. You love me. I'm sorry, I thought I was being cute, teasing you. I guess it was mean. I love you, and I am sorry," John said caringly.

He pulled me into him and kissed me.

"So, do you want to go?" he asked again.

"Yes, I want to go, and I still hate you," I replied, sniffling.

John laughed and gave me another kiss.

"I'm glad you want to go because I have already bought you a plane ticket."

"So you finally said, I love you," Ben said. Everyone cheered.

"Yes, we said it a couple of weeks ago," John replied to everyone.

"One more thing. I also bought you a ticket to Hawaii for October," John stated. "I love you, and you are stuck with me forever."

"Forever," I repeated with a large smile on my face.

"Yes, forever, you goofball," John said caringly.

John leaned in and gave me a tender kiss. The group made a childish noise. We laughed.

***

I had been to P-town many times before, but never with a significant other. The city is unique—free from hate and prejudice. People hold hands walking down the street, regardless of whether they are straight, gay, bi, lesbian, or trans.

There were many restaurants, shops, and nightclubs to visit throughout the week. The guys had the same tradition as I did—lunch at the Lobster Pot restaurant on our first day and again on our last day. We were all having a great time. I held onto John so everyone knew that this hot guy belonged to me and to keep their hands off him. I don't know if being around so many attractive guys who were only wearing shorts was making John insecure, but he dragged me back to the B&B at least once a day for a quickie, then back to the group. We weren't the only ones rushing back to the B&B for a quickie. We all had stressful jobs, so I think it was the lack of stress that made everyone extra horny.

On our last day, we rented bicycles and rode to the beach at the farthest point, where land ends. It was a warm early-September day, but not too humid. We played volleyball with anyone who would let us join. But mostly, we relaxed on the sand, joking around as we always do, and watched the men walk by in Speedos, rating them from one to ten according to the size of their bulge. We cheered as they walked past. Some said thank you, and others flipped us off, depending on their score. It was close to two p.m., and we hadn't eaten lunch yet. We were hungry and knew we wanted to go to the Lobster Pot.

We walked beside our bikes on the walking paths for a short while to enjoy the view. We heard some moaning off in the bushes and decided to investigate. One large animal in a leather harness was humping a smaller animal doggy style. The large animal waved hello while continuing to hump the smaller one. The things that happen in P-town.

***

Two months later, we were all off to Oahu, Hawaii. We had all been there before, so we mostly just relaxed on this trip. We all loved being in Hawaii. We spent each morning jogging on the beach or doing tai chi at sunrise. Everyone in the group liked to exercise, but it was just too beautiful outside to spend an hour each day inside at a gym. Mornings were the perfect time to get exercising out of the way, so as not to interfere with our daily activities, even if we hadn't planned any activities.

We decided to explore a waterfall that many people avoid because it requires a long hike to reach. Harry and Ben had heard about it from friends who had been there. It looked like something right out of a movie. The trail we took opened up to reveal a large pool of dark green water being fed by a thirty-foot-high spout. As the water fell, a mist resembling a cloud hovered near the falls. We had to be careful when walking around because the mist made the rocks slippery. A small cave sat behind the waterfall, where you could stand and look through the flowing water, but nothing on the other side was clear. The stone walls surrounding the falls were a dirty brown, covered in green trees and shrubbery growing up their sides with brightly colored flowers poking out here and there. It all took place under a beautiful blue sky.

We swam completely naked in the pond at the bottom of the waterfall. We had all seen each other naked in the locker room at the gym before, so there was nothing to be embarrassed about. And we weren't expecting any company because the path we took to get here was empty.

"Let's take a picture of us naked by the waterfall," John said.

"Okay," I replied.

Ben took the photos using his new digital camera, which he had bought just before the P-town trip. Ben, a professional photographer, posed us in various positions around the waterfall. I was getting excited, posing with John naked, and had to jump into the cold water. When I got out of the water, everyone was laughing at me. I went and hugged John and whispered in his ear.

"I wish you could fuck me behind the waterfall," I asked.

"Maybe before we leave," he replied, chuckling.

I had to jump back into the water again because any mention of having sex with John gave me a boner.

After our photo session, it was Ben and Harry's turn. Ben showed John how to work his camera. After them, it was now Carlos and Mike's turn, followed by Paul and Bob. Everyone knew how exciting it was at the beginning of a relationship, even at our age. So before we left, John asked the guys if we could have some privacy for a while behind the waterfall. The guys teased us as if we were teenage boys, "No problem, go have fun."

From behind the waterfall, we could hear the guys splashing around. It was exciting to have sex outdoors. I fell more in love with John as each day passed. I very seldom have to make the first move to initiate affection between us because John always beats me to the punch.

***

By our first anniversary of the day John and I met, I had moved in with him lock, stock, and barrel, and had rented out my condo. The only thing I missed about my condo was Marie. We had had many wonderful talks and dinners together over the past three years. We promised never to lose touch. Plus, I didn't need to worry about her because she was moving into the guest house at the home that her youngest son, Johnny, and his partner, Gabriel, had recently bought, so that she wouldn't be alone.

We celebrated our anniversary with a small party at John's house—or should I say our house—with close friends and immediate family. I always thought it was so cute when Bobby would hug and kiss his dad on the lips. My father wouldn't even hug me. Bobby came over to wish me a happy anniversary and told me how excited he was that I was going to be his second dad.

Bobby didn't understand the difference between a wedding and an anniversary, so he thought that his dad and I were now married. Bobby, now eight years old, jumped into my arms, gave me an enormous hug, and my first kiss on the lips, and said, "I am going to call you Pop."

I hugged Bobby tightly for several moments. He started fidgeting and said, "Let me go, Pop. I can't breathe."

"I'm sorry, Bobby," I said. Everyone was laughing at us.

"That's okay, Pop, I love you."

I kissed him on his cheek, and he said, "I need cake." We all laughed.

Alison stood in the middle of the family room but didn't say anything. John noticed her standing and asked, "Do you need to say something?"

Alison cleared her throat.

"Yes. Yes, I have something to tell everyone." The room fell silent. "Dave and I are getting married." Everyone but Bobby cheered.

"I know we've only been dating a few months, but we love each other, and we see no need to wait," Alison said excitedly.

Everyone rushed to congratulate both of them. Dave was a nice guy, and we all got along great as a family. He was on the quiet side, but with the right encouragement from everyone, we could coax him into opening up.

"He's not this quiet when we're off by ourselves," Alison said, smirking. Dave blushed.

I honestly don't think Dave is used to all the hugging and kissing that happens in this family, but to be honest, neither was I when I first met everyone. However, from the very beginning, when Bobby saw I was being quiet, he would take my hand and say, "Let's go play." Soon after, we became the same age, playing tag, having a catch in the backyard, or jumping into the pool at John's house, now our house.

The only family member struggling with Alison dating was Bobby. When Alison announced they were getting married, Bobby showed no excitement. He was used to having his mom all to himself. He didn't dislike Dave; he was just a little jealous of him.

"Why are you jealous of the time your mom spends with Dave? You weren't jealous of the time I spent with your dad when I first joined this family," I asked.

"You never took Dad away from me. You just came with us, and you've always paid a lot of attention to me, and you still do. That's why you're my best friend," Bobby explained.

I thought it was cute that he thought I joined him and his dad, and not the other way around.

I was talking with Bobby on the back patio, in the lounge chair where he was sitting in front of me, between my legs. I had my arms wrapped around him, hoping he felt safe. I'd been trying to help him better understand my insecurities, and how he was feeling right now was a great example of how I felt during one of those moments. He turned to look at me and said, "Oh! I think I understand."

Bobby was small for his age, but he was still growing at a

pace that made him too big to jump into my arms anymore. So, when he finished his turn, he lunged at me with his arms wide open to hug me. The back of the chair broke and collapsed with a loud thud. We both looked surprised, and we could hear Dad laughing from the kitchen. Bobby hugged me tightly and said, "I love you, Pop."

"I love you, too," I replied.

"Does Dave not pay any attention to you?" I asked Bobby.

"He's nice to me. He's not mean, but he doesn't pay attention to me like you do," Bobby replied.

"Do you want him to?" I added.

"Not really, I don't. I have you and Dad," Bobby explained.

I could see John smiling widely, standing by the sink at the kitchen window.

"You know your dad and I love you so much, Bobby. We are always here for you," I told him.

Bobby, still lying on top of me, gave me another big hug.

John, feeling a bit left out while looking out the kitchen window, said, "Hey, can I get one of those hugs?"

"Sure, Dad, come get one," Bobby replied.

Bobby stood on the lawn chair to equal his dad's height.

"Where's my hugs?" John asked.

Forgetting he was no longer a little boy, Bobby jumped into his dad's arms. John stumbled backward slightly but caught his balance by moving his left leg behind him so he didn't fall into the pool. Bobby hugged and kissed his dad.

"Pop, get up here and hug and kiss Dad. He feels left out," Bobby roared.

I stood up to hug and kiss them both. After a few hugs, both John and I tickled Bobby as he yelled and squealed for us to stop. We love that kid so much.

10

Chapter Ten

While Alison and Dave were in Maui for their honeymoon, the older three children were doing their own thing. But Bobby was still too young to be on his own, so John and I took him with us to Hawaii. Even though we were in Hawaii less than a year ago, Bobby thought it was fair for him to decide where to go on his vacation. Plus, John and I will use any excuse to visit Hawaii. However, we tend to spoil Bobby more than the other kids.

Bobby was at an age where he wanted constant attention from everyone around him. It was hard to find time for a romantic moment with John because Bobby wanted to be between us at all times during the trip. On the plane, he sat in the middle seat. When walking through the airport, he was in the middle of us, holding each of our hands.

When we stopped for a quick bite before heading to the hotel after landing in Oahu, Bobby needed to use the bathroom while John and I sat at the table. We thought I could sit on one side of John, and Bobby would sit on the other. But when Bobby returned, he paused, looked at us, and studied us. Then he grabbed a chair and placed it between John and me, telling me to scoot over. After sitting in his chair, he looked at both of us and said in his child voice, "Now, isn't that better?" We couldn't do anything but laugh.

"Yes, Bobby, that's better," John said.

I placed my hand on Bobby's head and messed up his hair. He looked at me and said sternly, "Pop. Please don't touch my hair." John and I chuckled.

After arriving at our hotel, which was directly across from Waikiki Beach, Bobby said he wanted to go to the beach right away. We told him that we needed to go to the room first, and then we could go to the beach. Even though Bobby had seen the ocean many times before living in California, he said that this ocean felt different here.

"This is an island with water all around it, and the only way to get off it is by boat or a plane. We are like pirates, aren't we?" Bobby stated excitedly.

John and I chuckled.

"Yes, we are like pirates," John replied.

We hadn't been in our rooms for five seconds when Bobby started tearing off his clothes and yelling for his swimsuit. John was going through Bobby's suitcase as quickly as possible so we wouldn't have a naked boy running through the hotel lobby, out the front door, and to the beach. Even though an eight-year-old can be exhausting, we loved him so much, and we laughed.

"Calm down, Bobby," John said. "Here's your suit. Pop, and I will be ready in five minutes."

Thirty seconds later, Bobby was knocking on our door, asking why we were taking so long. John grabbed the backpack filled with drinks, snacks, and lotions, while I took our beach towels. After a quick ride down in the elevator and out the front door of the hotel, Bobby held each of our hands as we crossed the street to the beach.

"Dad, Pop, pirate ships on the horizon," Bobby yelled as he pointed to all the different ships and boats out in the ocean.

"Should we prepare for battle?" I asked.

John had seen Bobby and me play together many times, so he just watched as we fell into our characters.

"Dad, come join us. Help us find weapons to fight off the dirty scoundrels," Bobby yelled.

"Come on, Dad." I chuckled.

"Tell me what to do, Captain!" John called out.

"Gather anything you can find to make a weapon out of," Bobby ordered.

There wasn't much in the way of pretend weapons, except for a few short sticks in the trash can by the sidewalk, which we used as swords. We marched back and forth on the beach while people watched us until Bobby announced.

"They're heading out to sea, mateys, so no battle today."

We were all in our swimsuits, ready for some fun in the water. John and I laughed as we nodded to each other. That was our signal to attack. We grabbed Bobby by his hands and feet and swung him into the ocean. He yelled and squealed as he flew through the air. When he landed, we ran over to him, and we all started splashing each other.

"Dad, Pop, you're mean," Bobby yelled.

John and I smiled at each other, and Bobby knew what was coming next. He tried to run away. We grabbed him again and swung him back into the ocean. Bobby laughed.

We hoped Bobby would take a nap before dinner since John and I were exhausted. Bobby agreed to take a nap.

"Okay, but only if you and Dad take one," Bobby said.

"Yes, Bobby, we also need a nap," John replied.

Bobby had an adjoining room to ours. After he settled in his room, we shut the door between us and climbed into our bed in our underwear. With a boy who rarely knocks before entering, we have to wear underwear when sleeping.

I finally had a moment alone with John. I hadn't hugged or kissed him all day, it seemed. After a few moments of kissing, hugging, and telling him I wanted him to play with my boner, he told me to wait until we took a shower before dinner. I let out a loud sigh in frustration because my boner was yelling at me that it needed some attention. Actually, it was my butt that needed the attention. We said I love you and went to sleep.

We woke up about an hour and fifteen minutes later to find Bobby standing beside our bed, tapping his dad on the head, saying, "I'm hungry, Dad."

I grabbed the sheet as soon as I heard Bobby's voice and pulled it over us because I could feel John's erection pressing into me from behind as he spooned me. John told Bobby to take a shower and said he would get clothes out for him to wear to dinner. As soon as John heard the water running in Bobby's shower, he grabbed my hand, dragged me to the bathroom, and locked the door.

"I need this just as much as you do, sweetheart," John said.

He grabbed my underwear, pulled them to my ankles, and bent me over the sink.

"Sorry, honey, but here I come," John announced. "No time for a warm-up," John added.

John lubed me up and entered me.

"I'm sorry, but I hope you're ready for me, honey," John announced again. "I need you right now, I'm getting blue balls." He chuckled. "It's been two days, and that's two days too long."

"I think we're okay. I made sure I was ready before our nap, so bang away," I said.

As John was pumping my butt, fucking me hard, the way I loved it in moments like that, we talked about dinner and where to take Bobby afterward. Conversations like that are typical when you have kids. It didn't distract us from what we were doing; it's just part of life with kids. And when John is inside me, there isn't much that will take his focus away from the end result. After our release, we felt the stress leave our bodies.

"I have to get clothes out for Bobby, and then I'll be back for my shower," John said.

A nap must have done us all some good because we felt relaxed.

After dinner, John and I sat on the beach while Bobby played with a couple of boys staying at our hotel. We watched the sunset on the horizon as the sky rapidly changed colors. As we watched Bobby play, John and I sat against a palm tree with a flat board attached to it. I sat in front of John, between his legs, with his arms wrapped around me. Bobby was giving us some alone time to be romantic, as he likes to call it.

Many times over the past year and a half, when Bobby saw John holding me, he would say, "Are you being romantic?"

John would tell him, "Yes, I am son, I am being romantic."

Bobby would smile and say, "That's nice," and then he'd go play.

When we returned to our hotel room, Bobby was so tired that he barely had enough energy to get into his PJs and climb into bed. John pulled the covers over him up to his neck and kissed him goodnight. John picked up Bobby's dirty clothes off the floor as I kissed Bobby's forehead goodnight. John and Alison had always kissed their children goodnight, even if their children were already asleep, and I continued doing the same with Bobby. Now it was our turn to climb into bed. John pulled me close to him and kissed my cheek.

"Having two children with you on vacation is tiresome and so much fun when one child is eight years old, and the other child is fifty-one years old," John giggled, and I laughed.

"Watching you and Bobby play together earlier today on the beach was breathtaking. Anyone watching the two of you for five minutes would understand why he calls you his best friend," John acknowledged.

"When you two have a conversation, you sometimes talk like children, and other times you speak like two adults. You are an amazing pair of human beings," John added.

I turned to face John, then looked at him in amazement as we settled into bed. He kissed me gently. I never thought anyone could love me like this man loved me.

"You need to prepare yourself for the day when Bobby gets older and no longer needs you like he does now," John said softly.

"I know how that feels because I went through it with Sam, Sarah, and Lisa. But more recently, I went through it with Bobby. He doesn't need me like he used to," John said.

"What do you mean he doesn't need you like he used to?" I asked, concerned.

"What Bobby and you have now is what Bobby and I used to have before I met you."

I could feel the tears welling up in my eyes, but I needed to hold it together until I figured out what John was talking about.

"I'm so sorry for taking that away from you. I never meant to hurt you like that," I said gently.

"It didn't hurt me, but it made me sad for a while." John took a deep breath.

"But after seeing what Bobby gave you, a son and a best friend, seeing how happy Bobby is when he is near you, I couldn't be any happier than I am right now."

John hugged me tightly as I wondered where all these emotions were coming from.

"Look at us all on vacation. Bobby wanted to be with us equally, not just you or me, but both of us together, the three of us. This trip is everything I could have ever wished for. I love you, and I am so thankful that you are my husband. Even though we can't be legally married, you are my husband."

John had tears running down his face. He didn't cry very often.

"I say thanks every day that you are in my life, Alex. I thank you for caring so much for our children, and especially Bobby. He loves you so much, and you love him back just as much," John continued.

Tears were flowing out of both of us as we held each other and cried a little softer.

"You love all our children, but you love Bobby like he is your own blood," John said as he looked lovingly into my eyes, and my heart took a few extra beats.

John is not an emotional person, unlike me, but for some reason, all these emotions came pouring out of him while the three of us were in Hawaii.

"Are you okay, sweetheart?" I asked caringly, as I sniffled.

"Why?" John asked.

"Well, isn't it my job to do all the crying in this family?"

"I thought I would give you a break," he snickered.

"I love you so much, Alex."

"I love you, too, you goofball," I said as I kissed his lips.

I felt so guilty about taking Bobby away from John. I didn't know what their relationship was like before I entered their lives. I was a little confused because I had never seen a father be so close to any of his children before. Bobby and I connected very quickly. John seemed so happy that I had Bobby in my life. But after John told me how pleased he was with how close the three of us had become on vacation, I started to wonder why and how it all happened.

While lying in bed facing each other in our underwear, I asked John, "Do you mind if I share my opinion on this matter?"

He smiled at me and said, "Go ahead."

He knew I was going to give my opinion no matter what he said. He knew me so well. If I didn't say what was on my mind, it would come bursting out of me at some point, and it would come out all wrong.

"I think when I came into your life, and with my insecurities, you became an adult again to Bobby. Before me, you were Bobby's buddy, his pal, and you could be the child he needed in his life after your divorce. But with you needing to be the adult in my life, I took you away from Bobby. You always say I'm just a big kid at heart. I would have given anything not to have taken Bobby away from you," I said, then exhaled deeply.

John lay next to me, listening, because he knew that if he had said anything, I would have lost my train of thought. John knew how to take such good care of me.

"Well, on this vacation, Bobby needs both of us because of the issues he's having with Dave coming into our family. Dave is a great guy, but he doesn't open up about things like most of us do. And he and Bobby have never warmed up to each other. But Dave is exactly what Alison needed in her life, and Bobby will come to see that someday."

Sometimes when I get philosophical and long-winded, John looks at me like I am full of shit and smiles. He knows I mean well.

"So, you slipped back into Bobby mode, his playmate, his buddy, just like you were before I came into your life. We're all about Bobby on this trip, and that's precisely what he needs. I think it's also what you and I both need. I know kids can sometimes push couples apart, but I believe Bobby brings us closer together."

"You grabbed my hand, dragged me to the bathroom, pulled down my underwear, and told me you needed me so badly. I love being needed by you that much. That told me everything I need to know about how much you care. And the best thing is, I don't think I'm using sex as a coping mechanism anymore. You show me every day how much you love me, even if you don't say the words."

"So, I think that because I am doing much better with my insecurities, you can stop being the adult for both of us all the time. But if I ever need you, I will let you know. This means, at least for a few more years, Bobby still needs the child in you, and I think we will both have him for a few more years until he grows too big for us."

"But don't worry, I will be a child until the day I die," I said.

John laughed.

"I will always need you, Alex."

"You can drag me into the bathroom and bend me over the sink anytime you want to," I said, grinning.

"Would you like to be romantic now?" John giggled.

"Yes, please," I replied.

John took me by my hand, led me straight to the bathroom, locked the door, pulled down my underwear to my ankles, bent me over the sink, lubed up my butt, and said, "I need you more than I have ever needed you in my entire life." He kissed the back of my neck.

"Can I please get inside you?" he asked as he kissed my neck once more, with his boner poking against the crack of my butt.

"Yes, please," I replied.

"Yes, sir. Whatever you want," John said with a slap to my ass.

As he entered me, there was a knock on the bathroom door.

"Not now," John whispered in my ear.

"Dad, can we go downstairs and get something to eat? I'm hungry," Bobby exclaimed.

"It's eleven o'clock, Bobby, go back to bed," John replied, frustrated.

"Dad," Bobby whined. "I'm hungry, and I can't sleep when I'm hungry."

John let out a frustrated moan, and I giggled.

"Go get dressed, and we'll be ready in five minutes," John said.

We knew Bobby went back to his room because we heard his TV turn on.

"Can we finish this when we get back?" John asked caringly.

"Don't forget where you left off, sir," I giggled. "It's not the first time we've had to stop in the middle of lovemaking to take care of Bobby, and it won't be the last."

We both laughed.

We looked at each other and said at the same time, "I love

that kid."

"And I love you," John said as he kissed me softly.

"And I love you too," I replied as I kissed him back.

11

Chapter Eleven

I wanted this trip to be a great experience and a lot of fun for everyone. I had never been on a helicopter, and before asking Bobby if he wanted to go up in one, we called Alison on Maui to get her approval.

"If Bobby wants to go, it's fine with me," she said.

"Would it be okay if we took him parasailing and ziplining?" John asked.

"Who is the bigger kid, Alex or Bobby?" Alison asked jokingly.

"It's a toss-up, but I am having such a great time." John chuckled.

Alison put Dave on speaker so we could all discuss the safety issues.

"As long as they have a good safety record, I don't see any problem," Dave said.

"I agree with Dave," John added.

The final decision about the kids was always up to Alison and John, but keeping open communication among all four of us was important as a family unit.

"We are having so much fun, and Bobby is being the best boy ever," I yelled out from across the room. Alison chuckled.

"We'll see you all a week from Sunday. Tell Bobby I love him," Alison added.

"I will send your love from both of you," John replied. "Bobby doesn't think Dave likes him."

"Tell Bobby we both send our love," Dave added. "And when we get home, I'll spend some more one-on-one time with him. I'm sorry. I'm not good at letting people know I care. I'm trying to get better at it."

"I know you are, Dave," John said. "But little boys need to be reassured about those things."

John ended the call.

We took Bobby out to lunch, where surfing lessons were happening. Bobby was jumping up and down excitedly as he watched the surfers stand on their boards and ride the waves to shore.

"Can I take a surfing lesson?" Bobby asked.

John and I would exchange a look when we were concerned about Bobby's safety and preferred not to discuss it in front of him.

"Not today, Bobby. Our schedule is full, and I don't think we have the time," John answered.

"Dang it," Bobby responded.

We had trouble keeping Bobby's attention on lunch with all the activities around us: people surfing, dogs chasing frisbees, people playing frisbee, and volleyball. However, as soon as we mentioned helicopter rides, we caught his interest.

"Finish eating your lunch, and we can go, son," John said. Bobby smiled.

We planned to spread out all our activities over several days to ensure we wouldn't have to rush through any of them. After lunch, we took out our laptop and watched videos of each activity to make sure none of them would be too scary for Bobby or me. John had nerves of steel.

Bobby was so excited about the helicopter ride and ziplining. He said the parasailing scared him because there was nothing to hold him in the seat. He was afraid of falling out.

After watching the videos, we scheduled our helicopter ride for the following evening. The ride would last fifty minutes, which included flying over Pearl Harbor, followed by a sunset view of Waikiki Beach. For the remainder of the day, we embarked on a tour of Pearl Harbor, visiting the museum, a ship, and the USS Arizona Memorial.

I pointed to the channel where the Navy ships and submarines enter.

"In 1975, my submarine came through the channel right over there after spending six months traveling around to different countries," I told Bobby.

We were standing on the Arizona Memorial while I was telling Bobby about my submarine.

"Are you a hero for being in the Navy?" Bobby asked.

"No, I just did my job," I replied.

"You're a hero to me, Pop," Bobby added.

Bobby gave me a big hug and told his dad to join in. John hugged us both tightly.

***

When we arrived at the airport for our helicopter ride the following day, an older man, a single rider, asked if he could join us. He had been sitting at the airport for a couple of hours, waiting for someone to say yes.

"I made a promise that I would take a ride, but I forgot to make a reservation," he said.

Bobby wanted the three of us to sit together, so the front seat next to the pilot remained empty. He seemed like a nice guy. Maybe a little sad, and a little lonely, but harmless.

The three of us looked at each other and nodded our heads.

"Sure, we'd be thrilled if you joined us," John acknowledged.

"Why are you by yourself?" Bobby asked the older man.

"Bobby, it's not appropriate to ask such personal questions," John responded.

"That's okay," the man replied.

"We should all introduce ourselves before we go for our ride," John interrupted.

"I'm John, this is my husband Alex, and this is our son, Bobby."

"I am Oliver, it is a pleasure to meet you all, and I am so glad that you are family," Oliver replied.

Bobby looked confused.

"I don't understand?" Bobby said.

"When someone acknowledges that you are family, gay people are telling you they are also gay," John explained to Bobby.

"Oh, like a secret code," Bobby replied.

"Something like that," John chuckled.

Oliver and I grinned at each other.

"My partner of thirty-five years and I had been planning this vacation for some time. He passed away a couple of months ago, and he made me promise that I would still go," Oliver said sadly.

"We are sorry for your loss," I said softly, and a little teary-eyed.

"Dad, I don't understand. What does that mean?" Bobby asked.

"Passed away means that someone died," John said.

Bobby walked up to Oliver and gave him a hug around his waist.

"Is it okay if I hug him back?" Oliver asked John, looking somewhat nervous.

"Bobby, are you okay if Oliver hugs you?" John asked.

"Sure, I like hugs," Bobby replied.

Bobby stood on a nearby cement divider to match Oliver's height, as he does for John and me, to get his hug.

Oliver hugged him back.

"Thank you, young man, I appreciate the hug," Oliver replied.

Bobby continued to ask Oliver questions.

"When is your anniversary?"

"Today would have been our thirty-fifth anniversary," Oliver replied.

What do you say in a moment like that? But Bobby rescued us.

"What's your husband's name?" Bobby asked.

"Bobby's a very inquisitive kid. Are you sure you're okay with all of his questions?" John asked caringly.

"I am fine. I love talking about Nick. His name is Nick," Oliver stated proudly.

"Because it is your anniversary ... oh wait. I have to ask first," Bobby said politely.

Bobby pulled John and me together and whispered, then looked back at Oliver and asked, "Would you like to have dinner with us all tonight for your anniversary?"

"It's okay," John acknowledged.

"Yes, young man, I would love to have dinner with you and your dad's," Oliver replied.

The helicopter ride was spectacular. We flew over Pearl Harbor and looked down at the ships and the Arizona Memorial, as Bobby excitedly told Oliver that his pop was in the Navy on a submarine.

The colors in the sky as we flew over Waikiki Beach were breathtaking. Bright oranges, reds, pinks, crimson, and golds painted the sky, creating a vibrant collage. But as we circled back to Pearl Harbor, we heard Oliver softly crying. John, Bobby, and I each placed a hand on his shoulder so he knew he wasn't alone.

After the ride, we all hugged Oliver and asked if there was a special place he wanted to eat dinner. He told us about the spot that he and Nick had planned to visit, and this time he had already made a reservation, so we jumped into a cab and headed out.

The restaurant was luxurious. The tables were draped with white linen tablecloths and set with elegant dishes and glassware, accompanied by more silverware than we had in our own kitchen. So we had to remind Bobby to behave himself.

"I always do," Bobby replied.

John and I laughed.

"Why so much silverware?" Bobby asked.

Oliver chuckled.

"Don't worry, Bobby. If you use the wrong one, the server will take away the correct one and replace the one you used," Oliver said.

"Thanks for telling us, Oliver. We've been to fancy restaurants before, but nothing this fancy," I said. John nodded in agreement.

For the next two hours, Oliver showed us pictures of Nick that he kept in his wallet and shared many stories about his life with Nick. He said they never took quick vacations; they always saved up for more exciting trips, like to London, Paris, and Hawaii. They had a wonderful life together. Oliver expressed how proud he and Nick were of their home in the Haight-Ashbury neighborhood of San Francisco, which they bought in their first year together.

After dinner, Oliver said he was tired and wanted to head back to his hotel. He thanked us for a wonderful afternoon and evening, mentioning that he was sure Nick was smiling down on us all for a fantastic anniversary celebration. We all knew that our meeting on this trip was something special and agreed to stay in touch. Oliver hugged everyone goodbye before getting into his cab.

When we got back to our hotel room, Bobby immediately climbed into bed. We had a busy day, and he was tired. After ensuring he was sound asleep, John quietly locked the door between the rooms and pulled me in close to hug me tightly.

"Are you okay, sweetheart?" John asked caringly. "I know how emotional you get over experiences like Oliver is going through."

We got undressed and climbed into bed, wrapped tightly around each other, with no underwear.

"Poor Oliver, thirty-five years. Please don't ever leave me," I said caringly.

"I don't plan on it, Alex, but we never know what's going to happen, do we?" John added, then kissed me lightly on my lips.

"I don't plan on us leaving each other till we are in our

nineties, old and wrinkled with a lot of grandchildren and great-grandchildren to say goodbye to us both," John said, smiling.

"Can you see me bending you over the sink at ninety, wrinkled old sagging butts?" John snickered.

I chuckled with that image flowing through my mind.

"Let's take a quick shower to wash the day off of us. Then I want us in the sixty-nine position so we can play around with each other, and then I want to get inside you for as long as we both can last. Please, pretty please with sugar on top," John asked in his pretend childish voice.

When John talks to me like I'm a child, he's telling me that he loves me more than anything else in life.

"I love you so much, John," I said softly.

"I love you, too, Pop," John replied. We both laughed.

"Okay, Dad," I added.

***

Our two weeks were almost over, and we were finally going ziplining. We had been looking forward to this day. There was a short classroom session that taught us how to buckle up and follow all the safety rules. Then we headed to the starting platform, where our guides prepared us for our flight. Bobby was small for his age, but he did meet the weight requirement to fly on his own. There was a lot of yelling and screaming as we sped through the air on a wire, surrounded by lush hills and a stunning waterfall. The three of us kids were having a great time, and Bobby was thoroughly enjoying the attention we were giving him. John and I loved giving him the attention he needed.

John was the first to fly so he could be on the platform to greet Bobby after his flight. John said he could hear Bobby screaming as he flew through the air. But John said the same about me as

I approached the platform.

"I want to do it again," Bobby yelled excitedly.

"Next time, Bobby. On our next trip to Hawaii, we will," John said.

"Oh, shucks," Bobby replied.

We all hugged to celebrate a successful flight, bouncing up and down like three little boys. People around us looked at us as if we were crazy.

***

To celebrate our last night, we went to a luau. Bobby sat between us and was bouncing all over the place, way too much sugar in that boy. Watching Bobby's face light up was entertainment all on its own. The food, the hula girls, and the fire dancers were fantastic. When the hula girls brought people up to dance with them, John and I pointed to Bobby. One of the dancers reached out for Bobby's hand and pulled him in front of the crowd. His eyes lit up so brightly.

Bobby wasn't a shy boy; he started wiggling all over the place to keep up with the dancer. I don't know who got more attention from the audience, Bobby, because he's just so dang cute, or the uncoordinated lady dancing next to him. We thought his face was going to split in half because of his broad smile. When the music changed tone, and the girl he was dancing with started shaking her hips super-fast, I thought Bobby's eyes would pop out of his head. He froze in place and stared at her hips. John and I laughed so hard we couldn't stop.

When the dancing was over, Bobby ran back to us and gave us both a big hug.

"You are the best dads ever," Bobby shouted. "Thanks, Dad, thanks, Pop, for everything."

"So you had a good vacation?" John asked Bobby.

"Oh my goodness, yes," Bobby replied.

"We did too," I added.

"Where are you taking me on my next vacation?" Bobby asked.

John and I chuckled.

"Where do you want to go?" John asked.

"I don't know, let me think about it," Bobby replied.

John and I exchanged a look, and Bobby understood precisely what it meant. We pulled him into a big hug and then tickled him until he squealed, "Uncle." We loved hearing him laugh. We annoyed some of the people nearby, but we didn't care; our boy was happy.

"We both love you so much. I hope you know that, son," John said as we both held him tightly.

"I love you, too, you goofballs," Bobby added. We all laughed.

12

Chapter Twelve

John and I struggled to let go of Bobby after we returned home from Hawaii. We became a close-knit family, just the three of us. We wished he could have come to live with us full-time. During those two weeks, John and Bobby's bond grew stronger, something John thought he had lost forever. The rekindled bond also brought John and me closer, and I didn't think we could get any closer.

Alison greeted us all at her front door, as Bobby jumped out of the car and ran to her.

"I'm home, I'm home," Bobby yelled.

"Yes, you are, my boy. I think the entire neighborhood knows you are home," Alison chuckled.

Bobby gave her several big kisses and a warm hug. Dave was standing behind her, waiting to greet us all in the entranceway. After hugging his mom, Bobby looked at Dave calmly and said hello, with neither of them attempting a hug.

Alison shut the front door as we all moved toward the family room at the rear of the house.

"Hello, Bobby. Did you have a good time in Hawaii?" Dave asked.

"Oh my god, did I ever," Bobby shouted.

John and I chuckled.

"It was the greatest two weeks of my life," Bobby said enthusiastically, with his hands flying through the air. Then he ran to his dad and gave him a big hug and kiss.

"Thanks, Dad, thanks for the wonderful time. Every kid should have a great dad like you. I love you so much."

"I love you, too, kiddo. I had a great time with you also," John replied.

Alison looked amazed at this display of emotions between them.

After Bobby let go of John, he jumped into my arms, giving me a big hug and a kiss, just like he always did. Dave looked sad, I think because he felt left out. Maybe he was realizing that if he wanted any attention from Bobby, he would need to show Bobby that he cared about him, too.

"Thanks for my vacation, Pop, and thanks for playing pirates with me on the beach," Bobby said joyously. Mom giggled.

"What else would best friends do for each other?" I replied.

Bobby hugged me one more time.

I whispered into Bobby's ear and said, "I think Dave is feeling a little left out of the hugs, so go give him one and tell him you're glad he and Mom had a great honeymoon. Okay, Bobby?"

Bobby looked at me and said, "Okay, Pop."

Bobby rushed over to Dave and wrapped his arms around his waist while standing next to Alison, surprising both of them.

"Welcome home," Bobby said. Dave smiled.

"Thanks, Bobby," Dave replied.

Everyone was grinning as Bobby ran off to his room.

As soon as John closed his driver-side door, he began crying softly, with his head tilted and resting on the steering wheel. John had never shown much physical emotion, but he often expressed his feelings with words. I took his hand and asked what was wrong.

"This is the part about being divorced that I have always hated. And after spending two weeks with Bobby, I feel like I have lost them all again. We were a family, the three of us, and I don't want to lose that," John exclaimed.

I was about to speak, but John interrupted me.

"I know what you are about to say, Alex, but the older kids don't need me anymore like they used to. They are young adults or nearly so. I am used to them not needing me as much. But Bobby needed me after the divorce. He was glued to my side, and I feel like I just got him back after the past two weeks," John said breathlessly.

I didn't know what to say to comfort him because I felt the same way. I wished Bobby were coming home with us, too. I held John until he stopped crying. As I was holding him, I saw Alison, looking out the living room window, watching us. From her point of view, she had to know John was crying. I lifted my head from John's shoulder to look at her, but she didn't look away. Maybe she understood what John was going through. It must have been tough on her, too, when any of the kids were gone for long periods.

"Is this what you feel like when you are having one of your insecure moments?" John asked.

"Yes, it is," I replied, and then kissed him on his cheek.

"If I have to be honest, I wish he were coming home with us, too," I added.

John looked up and kissed me with his wet, messy face and said, "Can I take you home and fuck you, please? It will make me feel better."

"Yes, John, you can." I chuckled.

This was the first time I hadn't cried during an emotional moment. I felt that I had to be strong so I could support him in his time of need. It's not often that John needs any support because he is the rock of our entire family, I thought. But how exhausting that must be. It felt good to be there for him and not fall apart myself. Maybe I can do that more often instead of becoming a total loser.

I told John in Hawaii that I didn't need him to be the adult in the room all the time. Perhaps when he mentioned Bobby in Hawaii, that was him asking for more support. So maybe I can be the adult when he needs one. Am I actually starting to like myself? Am I finally growing up? Maybe Dr. Smith was right; perhaps an old dog can learn new tricks.

"I'm here whenever you need me, John. To hold you, talk with you, make love to you, and cry with you," I said softly.

"A little less crying, please. For me, anyway. I hate when I cry," John said softly. "And I have to tell you, sir. Have you noticed how you are crying much less over the past three or four months? I am so proud of you," John said supportively.

"Really?" I asked.

"Yes, really," John responded.

We climbed into bed around nine p.m. because we had to return to work the next morning, and we were exhausted. We had already enjoyed some afternoon delight earlier in the day, so we were ready to sleep. John had just wrapped himself around my backside, and now that we were home without an eight-year-old to surprise us, we weren't wearing underwear. Tired or not, John had a boner pressing against me as he usually does most nights. I could tell John was about to fall asleep because his body twitched just before he did. I was seconds from sleep myself when John's cellphone rang. The caller ID read "Alison, landline," so we knew it was Bobby calling because Alison always uses her cell. John grabbed his phone from the nightstand.

"Hey Bobby, you okay?" John asked.

"Is Pop there with you?"

"Yes," John said sleepily. "We just crawled into bed."

"Are you being romantic?" Bobby asked. I chuckled.

"No, Bobby, we need to catch up on our sleep because we have to go back to work tomorrow," John replied.

"Are you on speaker so Pop can hear me?" Bobby muttered.

John clicked on the speaker icon. "Yes, it's on speaker ... Why are you calling so late?"

"I miss you and Pop," Bobby said softly.

"We miss you, too, buddy! We got so used to seeing you every day," John said as I pushed my face into his back.

"You are the best two dads that anyone could ever have," Bobby uttered.

"We love you too, so much," John said.

"We are always close by whenever you need us. You know that, son, don't you?" John responded, reassuringly.

"Yes, Dad, I know," Bobby replied.

"Will you come see me after work tomorrow, Dad and Pop?" Bobby asked.

"Yes, we will, but it might be later than usual because we have a lot of work to catch up on after being gone for two weeks,"

John stated.

"Didn't someone do your work for you while you were gone?"

"Well, we hope they did."

"Now go to sleep, and we'll see you tomorrow. And if you need us during the day, call us, okay?" John said in his dad tone of voice.

"Okay, Dad, Pop. I can go to sleep now," Bobby yawned.

John pressed the off icon with his finger.

John looked at me as I pulled my face out of his back and said, "Are you having an insecure moment?"

"Yes, I am. But can we stop calling it insecurity sex? I don't do that anymore," I replied, sniffling softly.

"How about making love to make both of us feel better?" John asked with a chuckle.

"You know me so well, John," I whispered into his left ear.

"Why are you whispering? No one can hear us."

"It seemed sexy," I replied, smiling.

"You're always sexy," John said.

"I love you, John."

"I love you, too, Alex."

13

Chapter Thirteen

On our second anniversary, John asked me to marry him. Of course, I shed a few tears—I'm not made of steel—and naturally, I said yes. John knew that I would love it if he made a grand gesture when he asked me the big question. Even though I knew we would be together forever, I once told him that I would be afraid to ask, just in case he said no. I had battled through many of my insecurities, but I hadn't won all my battles yet.

When John told Bobby that he was going to ask me to marry him, Bobby said he wanted to be part of the asking.

"Harry and Ben are throwing us an anniversary party this coming Saturday night at their house. So, Bobby and I are taking you to your favorite Italian restaurant, Marino's, in Toluca Lake on our anniversary to celebrate," John said.

"Just the three of us?" I asked.

"Yes, just the three of us," John replied.

When we entered, the host informed us that the only table available was located at the back of the restaurant, near the small banquet room.

"Is that table satisfactory for you, gentlemen?" the host asked.

"That's fine," John replied.

As the host guided us to our table, I heard voices that sounded familiar. As we got to the doorway of the banquet room, I looked inside, and everyone yelled, "Surprise!"

Bobby yelled, "Surprise, Pop!" as he stood beside me.

John kissed me on my cheek and said, "Happy anniversary, sweetheart."

All our family and close friends were there with large smiles on their faces. We sat down to eat after exchanging greetings with everyone. Dinner was served buffet-style. The menu included spaghetti and meatballs, lasagna, chicken Parmesan, eggplant Parmesan, fettuccine Alfredo, antipasto, and tiramisu for dessert. Bobby was fidgety throughout dinner because he couldn't wait for John to pop the question.

As soon as we finished our dessert, Bobby asked, "Is it time, Dad?"

"Is it time for what?" I asked, looking curiously at John.

Bobby had a large smile on his face.

"You aren't going to make me cry in the restaurant, are you?" I asked John with my face all crinkled up.

"Well, yes, I am," John said lovingly.

"I could make a big speech, but I don't think I have to tell you how much we all love you," John said, grinning.

I was holding my breath, trying not to cry. I couldn't believe that just two years ago, I didn't know a single person who truly loved me, and I didn't believe there was anyone who did. But now I had an entire room full of people who did love me, and it was all because of John. John said it was all me who did the hard work and he was just my leaning post. Outside the banquet room, people were turning around in their chairs to watch us.

"Come on, Dad," Bobby encouraged.

I was still holding my breath, not knowing exactly what was going on.

"I'm getting there, Bobby," John said as he tried his best to calm him down and keep him from bouncing.

John placed his hands on Bobby's shoulders. This seemed to help him relax.

"When I told Bobby I was going to ask you something tonight, he said he wanted to be part of the asking. So we both decided to take you out to dinner, and after I told Ben and Harry what we planned to do, well, as you can see, the dinner party grew," John explained. "So this is our anniversary party we were supposed to have this coming Saturday night."

John knelt on one knee, with Bobby standing behind him, holding his shoulders and shaking him so much he nearly toppled over. I was so shocked that my mouth was wide open as I tried to catch my breath.

"So, with the approval of the entire family ... would you marry me?" John asked softly.

I felt a lump in my throat so big I couldn't speak, so I nodded yes as tears streamed down my face.

Marie handed me a handkerchief to wipe my eyes when she said, "I have a container of cannoli in my car. Don't forget to take them home with you tonight."

I looked up and smiled broadly at her while everyone else was laughing. I love that little Italian lady. Bobby didn't lose focus on his dad.

"The rings, Dad. Don't forget the rings!" Bobby said excitedly.

"I'm getting there, kiddo."

John pulled a small felt bag out of his front pocket, which held the rings. I released a deep breath.

"I hope you like the rings we picked out. These were the ones that Bobby liked best because he said you don't like gaudy jewelry, and I agreed," John said nervously.

"The rings are small silver bands that we will wear as engagement rings and will be replaced with wider silver bands on the day of our commitment ceremony."

John took a deep breath.

"I know that someday, or I hope that someday, we can be legally married, but I can't wait that long. I need to make you mine, now," John said, his smile so wide that I thought his face was going to split.

"I'm already yours," I replied, my heart beating fast.

"Yes, you are," John said, smiling.

John slid my ring onto my finger and then handed me his ring to put on his. I was so nervous I dropped it, but I caught it midair. Everyone gasped and then clapped. When I stood up to kiss and hug John, I pulled him up with me from his kneeling position. Bobby stepped between us, and we accidentally crushed him a little. We moved back a bit so he could jump up and down while I leaned over him to kiss John.

Bobby roared, "Dad's going to marry Pop!"

Bobby stood on a chair to match our height so he could get hugs and kisses from both of us. Bobby may have looked like a younger version of John, but as an adult, I think he will be a little shorter. People in the restaurant clapped and cheered for us, along with everyone in the banquet room.

We planned to hold a ceremony in mid-May at a park in Pasadena when the flowers would be in full bloom. The spot we chose was where many weddings are held each year.

It had been several months since Alison and Dave got married. However, when it came to Dave, Bobby was still a little reserved about showing any affection. But Dave wasn't opening up to Bobby either. Dave is perfect for Alison; they are deeply in love, but Dave struggled to relate to younger children. He told us that his father was not an affectionate man.

"He was a kind man and took great care of us by providing everything we needed, such as clothing, shelter, medical care, and food—but he wasn't affectionate to my sister or me," Dave had acknowledged wistfully.

Since we returned from Hawaii last year, Bobby had been spending more time at our house than at his mom's house. It wasn't something we planned; it just naturally happened.

***

Today is our commitment ceremony, and I'm pleasantly surprised with breakfast in bed from Bobby and John. Bobby stayed at our house last night and helped his dad make breakfast, so I wasn't greeted by morning sex like I usually am on special days. Bobby and John were still in their pajamas as they brought breakfast to me on a tray. They both had big smiles on their faces. Bobby yelled, "Happy commitment day, Pop."

I'm not fond of the word *commitment.* It made me feel as if I were being committed to an insane asylum. I had to laugh when Bobby said it.

Before John placed my breakfast tray in front of me, Bobby jumped onto the bed and hugged me. And now, at nine years old, the bed bounces more than when he was seven. My tray held enough food for three people, so I assumed I would have company joining me for breakfast. John leaned over and kissed me before sitting next to me.

"Happy commitment day, Pop," John said, smiling.

"I love you two so much," I exclaimed, chuckling.

In unison, John and Bobby replied, "We love you, too."

We sat quietly on the bed, picking food off the tray and shoving whatever we grabbed into our mouths. Well, maybe not so quiet. With all the sounds we made enjoying our food—yum, mmm, slurp, crunch—and a burp from Bobby.

"Bobby," John yelled out.

"Sorry, Dad, it slipped out." Bobby laughed.

"Well," Bobby said with a chuckle, "we learned in school last week that it is polite to belch after a good meal in China, Turkey, and India."

"Well," John growled, "we don't live in China, Turkey, or India, and we don't belch when others are eating. You know, Pop gets grossed out easily." We all chuckled.

I held onto the tray so nothing spilled.

"Sorry, Pop," Bobby said apologetically.

"Dad's right, it's gross," I added, smiling.

"Okay," John said sternly. "No more burping during meal time."

John got off the bed and opened the sliding doors to the patio. A nice, cool morning breeze filled the room with the scent of eucalyptus from the backyard.

Bobby was giggling, so John took the tray of food from the bed and placed it on the floor. Bobby knew what was coming next because John gave me the look.

"Dad, Pop, don't you dare."

I attacked from one side, and John attacked from the other.

"It's time for a tickle fest," I yelled.

John and I tickled him until he begged for mercy. The sounds that came from that boy—the giggles, the laughter, the squeals.

"Dad, Pop, stop it!" Bobby laughed.

We carried Bobby like a hammock to the pool through the sliding doors. John held his feet, and I had his arms. We swung him back and forth while he kept laughing. When we released him, he shot into the air and splashed down like a cannonball. As soon as his head was above water, John and I jumped in, still in our PJs. We splashed each other until Bobby yelled, "I'm still hungry." God, that boy can eat!

I climbed out of the pool, grabbed a towel from a lounge chair, and semi-dried myself. I went into the bedroom, changed into a pair of boxers, and took the tray of leftover food outside onto the patio. Bobby and John semi-dried themselves with the towels I handed them, and we finished eating the cold eggs, bacon, sausage, and French toast. It isn't the first time we've had to eat cold food because the three of us got sidetracked by our goofing around.

We washed the breakfast dishes and made the beds. It was time for showers and to get dressed for the day's event. Before John went into Bobby's room to get his clothes ready, he whispered in my ear, "I missed waking you up this morning, so why don't I meet you in the shower in ten minutes for a quickie before we take ours?"

"Excellent idea, I missed you too this morning," I replied. "I'll be ready and waiting for you."

After John finished helping Bobby with all his clothes, I heard our bedroom door close and lock. As he entered the bathroom with his appendage pointing at me, he was ready to attack. I smiled.

"Good morning," I said again.

***

We hired the biggest stretch limousine available for the day, which could accommodate up to ten people for travel to the ceremony. John's oldest son, Sam, was his best man, and Bobby was mine. If I had not asked Bobby to be my best man, he would have been hurt so badly, and I would have lost him forever, I believe.

I think Bobby was more excited than we were about the day's events, and we were both ecstatic. Ben, Harry, Paul, Bob, Carlos, and Mike met us at our house around noon so we could all ride together in the limo. The day wouldn't have been complete without the guys with us. We did the same when each of them had their commitment ceremonies over the past couple of years.

The ceremony and reception took place near the greenhouse. The surrounding areas were adorned with vibrant flowers. A large tent with tables and a dance floor was set up near the garden area. Even though it was mid-May when the weather can be iffy, it was a beautiful sunny day, and the temperature was eighty-two degrees with a mild breeze.

John told me, "I ordered it just for you." I hugged him tightly.

John was fussing over me just how I always wanted. Every moment of the day turned into a bit of surprise. John planned everything, and all I had to do was show up.

"Am I doing enough to make this day memorable for you?" I asked.

"Every day with you in my life is special as long as you are happy," he said, his face lit with the most beautiful smile.

Of course, I became teary-eyed. You'd have to be a stone wall not to. Fortunately, I'm not a woman, because my makeup would have been a mess.

We didn't walk down the aisle because I thought I might pass out from nerves. We entered from the sides near the front, where the minister was waiting for us. John entered with Sam, following behind him, and Bobby was holding my hand, walking beside me. Chairs were set up in the garden area for fifty friends and family. Bobby stood with me on my side, and Sam stood with John on his. Sam looked over at Bobby and gave him a thumbs-up for taking such good care of me. Bobby returned the thumbs-up and smiled widely.

As we stood in front of the minister, Bobby was still holding my hand, which put Bobby between John and me. I tried to guide him back to my other side so I could hold John's hand, but Bobby wouldn't move. So there he stayed. A soft giggle flowed throughout the crowd.

Sam moved closer to his dad so he wouldn't be left out, and the minister welcomed everyone to the ceremony.

"We are here today to celebrate love between these two men, or should I say two-and-a-half men." Everyone chuckled again.

"Well, let's just say it's a family affair today," I added cheerfully.

I didn't cry like I used to, but I was teary-eyed. I gathered myself so everyone could hear and understand my vows to John. I cleared my throat.

"The day I met you was the luckiest day of my life. I have always struggled to trust people, but you have consistently shown me that I can truly trust you with my life. Through all my insecurities, and there were many, you never gave up on me. Then, as I got to know all of your friends — Paul, Bob, Carlos, Mike, Harry, and Ben — you introduced me to the friends I have always wanted. You guys mean the world to me." I turned my head to look at them. "And to our family, the commitment I make today is not only to you, John, but to our family as well. I love you all, and thank you for letting me be part of your family. A family like this is something I thought I'd never have. And to my little buddy, Bobby, thank you for always being there when I need you."

I took a deep breath.

"I love you, John," I said breathlessly. "I love you more than I can express, because I don't think there are enough words in the English language to describe how much I love you. I hope I can give back what you give to me to make me the happiest man in the world." I released a deep sigh.

"Can I cry now?" I asked, sniffling. "I can't hold it back any longer."

People in the crowd yelled "Yes" and then chuckled. Bobby let go of John and hugged me around my waist. When Bobby released me from his hug, I pulled him against me so we could both face John as he spoke.

"From the moment I met you, I knew I was going to spend the rest of my life with you. No matter how much you tried to chase me away with all your insecurities, and even the morning after we met, when you said you didn't want to see me anymore. I knew you didn't mean it. You were just scared of being hurt again. You started to cry that night, and when I asked if something was wrong, you told me it was because you were so happy at that moment, and I knew that I wanted to make you happy for the rest of your life."

John took a breath.

"So, I commit to you on this day, that I will do my very best, from the depths of my heart, that I will do everything in my power to give you the best life possible, for the rest of your life.

You fit perfectly next to me, and I wouldn't know how to live without you by my side," John said breathlessly.

"And me," Bobby yelled. Everyone laughed.

"Yes, you too, Bobby," John said, chuckling.

"I love you just how you are, Alex, and I would not change a thing about you. I know my family loves you, or I will say, how our family loves you."

Bobby was shaking his head yes, with a big smile.

"So again, I commit to you today, with all my love until my very last breath. I love you, Alex," John said, inhaling a long breath.

Bobby was yelling, "Are they married yet?"

"Not yet," said the minister, "We have to do the rings first."

"Oh .... I forgot," Bobby replied. The crowd snickered.

"Can I have the rings, please?" the minister asked.

Sam placed his ring into the minister's hand, and then Bobby put his ring into the minister's other hand.

"Please take the appropriate ring and place it on each other's finger and repeat these words. With this ring, I commit my love to you for the rest of my life," the minister said.

"With this ring, I commit my love to you for the rest of my life," we both said, teary-eyed and smiling.

"Wait one more minute?" the minister told Bobby.

"Okay," Bobby answered.

"I now pronounce you husband and husband. You may now kiss your husband," the minister added.

As John and I tried to kiss, Bobby excitedly jumped between us. John pulled in Sam, and we shared a four-way hug.

As we turned to walk down the aisle, the music from the reception area started playing. Bobby was holding Sam's hand and bouncing around as the guests stood and clapped for us while we passed by. The first group approaching us near the reception area was our family, so we could all hug and kiss each other. Dave was standing a little off to the side, and Bobby called out to him to join us. As he moved closer, John and I pulled him between us for a hug and kiss. I kissed Dave on one cheek, and John kissed him on the other. Alison was watching and laughing as Dave turned bright red. She pulled Dave close and kissed him, then said, "I love you."

After dinner was finished, the center table where everyone was sitting was cleared away so dancing could start. The first dance was for John and me, but Bobby wanted to join in. Alison reached out to take his hand in an attempt to pull him back.

"The first dance is only meant for the two people getting married," she said. He frowned.

When the second song started, it was a tune everyone could dance to. Bobby ran over to John and me, took our hands, and the three of us began dancing together. John signaled for our friends and family to join us.

"Bobby, go drag Dave onto the dance floor to join the family," I said.

Dave kept shaking his head no as Bobby pulled him onto the dance floor. Alison wrapped her arms around him as the music shifted to a slow tune.

"Is that better?" she asked.

"Yes, it is," Dave replied. "You know I only like to dance when I can put my arms around you."

"Me too," she added.

Bobby decided to get some cake when the slow dancing started.

As John and I danced with his arms wrapped around me, he told me we're going to Niagara Falls for a week starting in the morning. I had always wanted to visit Niagara Falls for a romantic honeymoon. John was making all my dreams come true. I told him once what my dream wedding would look like. We didn't discuss ahead of time where we would go; John said he wanted to surprise me, and he did.

14

Chapter Fourteen

Most gay couples celebrate their anniversary from the day they met, but with civil unions in the mix, which are legal in only some states, do we celebrate both dates or just the civil union? I guess it's a personal choice. John and I have decided to celebrate both of our anniversaries—any excuse for a party. On the day we celebrated our second civil union anniversary, we had been together for a total of four years and four months.

For the most part, many of my insecurities have disappeared. It's all because of John. He is my man of steel, my rock, my everything. Sometimes he treats me like one of his kids, teaching me right from wrong and how to handle different situations. I had to be retrained, and with four kids, he had the proper training for the job. However, from time to time, they reappear, and John comforts me by making love to me. I'm not using sex as a coping mechanism anymore, but sex does help calm my anxiety. And I love making love with my husband.

Our family continues to grow, and I'm amazed at how fortunate I am. Sam and his wife, Susie, who married right out of college two years ago, just had their second child, a little girl this time. John's oldest daughter, Lisa, got married a year ago, and they recently had their first child, a baby girl. They both live about thirty minutes away from us. We added a crib and two child-size beds to one of the bedrooms for when they stay overnight. Traveling with small children late at night is just not feasible, and I will find any excuse to let them stay.

When I first joined the family, the older three kids initially called me Alex, but when Bobby started calling me Pop, the others followed suit shortly after, mainly because Bobby put up a fuss if they didn't. Bobby did the same when I met our first grandchild. Bobby took me by the hand and led me to his crib, where he introduced me.

"Pop, this is Sam Jr., and Sam, this is Gramps," Bobby said happily. And yes, I got teary-eyed. They came from an overabundance of joy, nothing else. I hope the title of Gramps continues with all future grandchildren.

Sarah will graduate from high school in just a few days. Sarah is John's third child. Everyone in the family had numerous tasks to complete to ensure the graduation party would go off without a hitch. That meant that Bobby had to stay home with Dave. Since Alison and Dave had been married, Dave had never been placed in charge of Bobby for an entire day. Even after living in the same house with Bobby for two years, Dave had not developed a deeper relationship with Bobby. They liked each other and were polite, but no real bond formed. Both John and I had to work, so neither one of us was able to watch Bobby while Alison did last-minute errands.

School was already out for the summer. Bobby loved summer

vacation because all the sports he loved took place during the summer months. He was playing outside at the front of the house with many of the other neighborhood kids. When the kids were playing outside, there were always a couple of adults supervising, so Dave thought it would be okay to stay in the house and work in his home office. The street was quiet with minimal traffic, allowing the kids to ride their bicycles safely. They knew to move over to the side of the road if a car wanted to drive through.

It was street cleaning day, so one side of the street was free of cars. That gave the kids more space to ride their bikes. One of the teenagers from down the road, with loud rumbling mufflers on his car, drove a little too fast toward the kids, which excited them. When Dave heard the noisy car, he opened the front door to check on Bobby. All the kids had moved to the side of the road, but, for some reason, Bobby decided he wanted to race the car. As the noisy vehicle came roaring down the street, Bobby pedaled as fast as he could to beat it. The teenager didn't slow down or notice Bobby.

When Dave opened the front door, he saw Bobby pedaling hard, his rear end raised off the seat to get more momentum. Bobby was directly in front of the house as Dave walked out onto the front porch. Where Dave was standing, it didn't look like Bobby had any room between the car and the curb. Dave's heart was racing. He didn't yell at Bobby until the car had passed because he didn't want to scare him and cause something to happen. As soon as Dave knew Bobby was safe, he shouted in a stern voice.

"Bobby, get into the house, now."

Many of the kids and a couple of parents watched as Bobby rode his bike into his front yard and let it fall to its side in anger.

Dave, trying to hold his temper, told Bobby as he stood on the first step of the front porch.

"Get in the house and go to your room."

Bobby didn't understand what he had done wrong and thought Dave was just being mean.

"Why are you being mean to me?" Bobby yelled.

Dave told him again, "Go to your room until your mother gets home."

Bobby entered the house, stomping his feet as he climbed the steps to his bedroom.

Dave called Alison on her cell phone in a panic about what had just happened, stating that she needed to come home.

Before going into his room, Bobby called his dad from the upstairs hallway phone.

"Dave is being mean to me, and Mom isn't home," Bobby yelled.

"What happened?" John asked calmly.

"I was riding my bike and he yelled at me and told me to go to my room," Bobby growled.

John knew there had to be more to the story, so he told Bobby that he and Pop would be over as soon as they could. Bobby locked his bedroom door so no one could get in. Dave knocked on his bedroom door to talk to him after he had calmed down some.

"I'll open it when Dad and Pop get here," Bobby yelled.

Alison and Dave sat in the family room talking about what had happened. Dave explained that Bobby had scared him, and he didn't want to say something wrong or regret it later.

"I knocked on his door after I calmed down, but he wouldn't open it," Dave said.

Alison hugged Dave because she could see he was upset.

When Bobby got into trouble like any kid can, I always stood by quietly and listened to his parents and didn't say anything unless I was asked. Too many people talking at once can get confusing, even if Bobby wanted me to say something.

John brought Bobby into the family room, where we all sat and talked. Bobby came running over to me, but he knew the drill for when he got into trouble.

"Go sit in the single chair," I told him. He frowned.

Alison and Dave sat on one side of Bobby, and John and I sat on the other side on separate sofas.

"Bobby, do you know why we are having this family conference?" Alison asked.

"No. I was riding my bike and Dave yelled at me!" Bobby yelled.

"Don't shout, Bobby. You know shouting doesn't help matters," Alison added.

Bobby started crying softly. He always felt that he was being ganged up on whenever he got into trouble. But I think all kids feel that way. I always wanted to hug and protect him, but if I ever tried, John would give me the look, and I knew to stay sitting beside him. John had told me many times before that Bobby needs to learn right from wrong, so I shouldn't continually baby him. I was hearing John use some of the exact words on Bobby that he used on me over the years, helping me with my insecurity issues.

After Bobby told us all what he thought he was doing on his bike, Alison asked Dave to explain what he saw happening outside. Dave was nervous as he explained why he got upset with Bobby. Until this point, neither John nor I knew just what had happened.

"When I opened the front door, Bobby was racing a car down

the street while the other kids had moved to the side of the road. I waited for Bobby to be in a safe spot and then told him to come inside and go to his room," Dave said, taking a deep breath while looking at Alison.

Bobby said again, "I don't understand. Dave was just being mean because he doesn't like me!"

"You're wrong, Bobby. I do care about you. I love you," Dave added.

"No, you don't. You don't care about me," Bobby shouted.

"Bobby, Dave does care about you," John said.

"Then why doesn't he pay any attention to me?" Bobby asked. Dave didn't respond.

I wanted to comfort Bobby, but I also felt bad for Dave. Dave didn't know how to open up and share his feelings like we all did, and Bobby was used to that from the adults around him.

Alison was just about to say something when I spoke up.

"I don't know if I am going to say this appropriately, but I will try my best. Dave, I know you're not an outsider, but perhaps you still feel like one when it comes to Bobby. You two haven't really warmed up to each other, even after all this time. It didn't take me long with Bobby because in a way, he and I are the same age," I said.

John and Alison chuckled slightly and then stopped abruptly. I frowned at John.

"So why don't you talk directly to Bobby about how you feel about what happened today? And Bobby, I want you to sit still and listen until Dave is finished talking, not thinking about what you want to say back to him, sit there and listen. Can you do that for me, please?" I asked slowly so I knew Bobby was listening.

Bobby looked at me with a frown, and I frowned back at him.

"Yes, Pop, I can."

Dave took a deep breath.

"Bobby, when I opened the front door, you were pedaling your bike as fast as you could to keep up with that car." Bobby frowned. "You know you were," Dave added. Bobby's frown disappeared because he knew Dave was telling the truth.

"All of the other kids knew to go to the side of the road. And I can't believe none of the parents out there didn't yell for you to get off the road. If that car lost control and hit you, or you would have lost control of your bike ... well ...," Dave paused a moment.

"You could have been seriously hurt or even killed today. Do you have any idea of the pain we would all be in right this minute if you were no longer here with us?" Dave exhaled.

Dave is not an emotional guy, but his eyes began to well up. Alison placed her hand on his knee to comfort him. We looked at each other in amazement.

"We want you to be safe ... I want you to be safe. Whether you believe me or not, Bobby, I love you ... I may not show it, and I know I should, but I do love you, and you are very important to me." Dave released a breath as he attempted to hold back his tears.

Everyone in the room was teary-eyed, as we have been many times before in these situations with Bobby. Well, all except for Dave. Bobby jumped out of his chair, crying, ran, and jumped into Dave's arms.

"I'm sorry, I won't do it again, I promise," Bobby said.

Bobby held onto Dave tightly.

Bobby looked up at Dave and said, "I love you, too," and latched onto Dave again.

After more hugging and sniffles, Bobby looks at Dave and

said, "Am I still getting punished?"

Dave held Bobby's head with both hands, looked directly into his eyes, and said, "Yes, you are, young man." Bobby frowned.

"We'll talk about it and tell you your punishment after dinner," Dave said gently. "But for now, go to your room so we can all discuss it, please."

Bobby hugged everyone before heading to his room. As he walked away, Dave said, "No video games." Bobby frowned.

Before discussing Bobby's punishment, we ordered delivery from the Italian restaurant down the street, not my favorite Italian place.

"Are you okay, Dave? You never get emotional, and you scared me," I said with care.

"No," Dave replied, exhaling. "Bobby scared the crap out of me today. And today is the first time he said he loved me, and now I don't want to punish him."

"Is today the first time you said you love him?" I asked.

Dave hesitated and said, "Yes, it is, I'm ashamed to say."

You know you married into an entire family, not just Alison?" I added.

"I'm slowly figuring that out. I guess I need to work on my issues the same way you have been working on your issues over the years," Dave said softly. I nodded my head yes.

"Well, that's all Bobby wanted to know, that you love him. That's why he thought you didn't like him. Kids are strange that way," I added. We all exhaled a deep breath.

"I wonder what my life would have been like if my dad could have said those three simple words. I love you. Why are they so hard for people to say?" I said sadly.

John pulled me close and held me tightly.

"Now, getting back to his punishment, you have to," John

said caringly. “We all have to do it when he misbehaves, and Alex hates to punish him more than any of us.”

I shook my head in agreement with John.

“I do love that kid,” Dave added.

“We know you do,” Alison said caringly. She gently kissed his lips.

“And now Bobby knows you love him, too,” John added.

“What he did was bad, so how do I punish him?” Dave asked.

“After two years, you haven’t learned yet how we punish the kids?” John asked.

“No, I don’t pay attention to all that stuff. I leave it up to Alison.”

We all chuckled.

“He learns things quickly, so we are never too severe with our punishments. We normally take something away from him for a few days,” John added.

“But I want him to understand what he did wrong,” Dave replied.

“He already does,” Alison said.

“How do you know that?” Dave asked curiously.

“He stopped yelling at us,” Alison added, chuckling.

“Oh.” Dave smiled.

Alison teased Dave in front of John and me about his crying.

“My baby cried, I love you so much,” Alison teased.

“I love you, too,” replied Dave. We all laughed.

Dave looked at everyone with a crooked grin on his face and said, “Oh my god, I am turning into you people.” We laughed.

The doorbell rang with our dinner. Bobby ran out of his room and down the stairs. He hugged Dave and said, “I’m sorry, Dave.” He squeezed Dave around his waist one more time before he roared, “I’m hungry.” We all laughed.

15

Chapter Fifteen

Sarah's high school graduation day had arrived, and she was so excited. John was beaming like a proud papa should be. She had worked hard over the past four years to finish in the top ten of her class. In September, she would start classes at a nearby college. We love that all the kids chose to stay close to home as they continued their education.

Our family occupied an entire row at the graduation ceremony. Grandparents, aunts and uncles, nephews and nieces, brothers, and one sister, and no babies attended. I had a big smile on my face because I couldn't believe how lucky I was to have such a large and loving family.

The ceremony took place at the school's football stadium, where there is ample parking for family and guests' cars, as well as seating in the stands for everyone. Late May is the perfect time for an outdoor event when the weather hovers near eighty degrees. A stage was constructed in the center of the field, where speeches were made, and students were presented with their diplomas. With more than three hundred graduating students, multiple presenters passed out the diplomas as their names were called.

Applause and cheers erupted as families heard their children's names. When Sarah Montgomery's name echoed over the loudspeakers, our family cheered louder than anyone else had. At the end of the ceremony, the students tossed their caps into the air and erupted in cheers. Bobby was standing on the bleacher seat, holding John's and my shoulders so he could see over the heads in front of him as everyone applauded for the students.

After the ceremony, people were milling around on the field, talking with other parents and friends. I was standing with my back to John, chatting with a couple of our neighbors, when I overheard him greet someone he worked with. The voice sounded familiar, but I shrugged it off and kept talking to our neighbors.

"Hey, I haven't seen you since Friday," John said with a chuckle.

"John, this is my wife, Barbara. And this is John, we work together," the man said.

"Nice to meet you, Barbara," John added.

John turned and whispered to me. "When you're done talking, I have someone I want you to meet."

"Your husband needs you, so that's our cue to leave. We have to find Harry. We're meeting his grandparents for dinner to celebrate his graduation. They didn't come because they're not as mobile as they used to be," the neighbor stated.

I turned around to see who John was talking to. The panic that overtook my body was overwhelming. The man standing with his wife was Mark, the man I had an affair with before I met John. They were standing in front of John with their daughter, who had also just graduated from the same high school. When they'd called out the name Debbie McBride, I hadn't thought of Mark because he lived an hour away from us, or so I believed. We recognized each other immediately. We didn't say a word to each other. I was in shock, and so was he, if I read his face correctly.

"Mom, I don't want to listen to another adult conversation, so I'm going to go talk with my friends by the stage. I'll wait for you and Dad there," Debbie said.

"Okay," Barbara replied.

"Alex, this is Mark and his wife Barbara. I've worked with Mark for several years. This is my husband, Alex," John stated happily.

I nodded my head toward Barbara to acknowledge her, but I said nothing. My throat was frozen shut. I focused on her for a moment to see whether she recognized me, but she said nothing.

"We had our commitment ceremony two years ago," John acknowledged.

Mark knew that John was married to a man, but not to whom. Neither Mark nor I reached out to shake hands. John looked at me curiously. I just kept staring at Mark. He looked so much older, heavier, and sadder than I remembered him to be. John found my reaction strange. I could see it on his face, but he didn't ask why at the time.

I had a surge of emotions, recalling what I thought Mark meant to me years ago, but it wasn't like I still had those feelings; I felt more of a sadness for him, a sadness reflected in the numbness I saw in his eyes. I felt tears welling up, but held my breath to stop them. John knew what was happening to me.

"Are you okay?" John asked softly.

"I'm fine," I replied, taking a deep breath.

John probably thought my watery eyes were from all the excitement building up during the day. Just because I'd worked through many of my insecurities didn't mean I wouldn't get emotional. I exhaled a deep breath.

"When did you meet your husband?" Barbara asked John.

I held John's hand for emotional support. John squeezed my hand, then kissed my cheek.

"We met about four and a half years ago after some jerk dumped him," John replied.

Mark had a panicked look on his face, not knowing what else John was going to say.

"They had just returned after a weekend fishing trip. Alex thought everything was going well because they had such a great time together, or so he thought. The guy drove away after dropping him off at his condo and never contacted him again. So luckily for me, I met Alex about four weeks later and we've been together ever since," John exclaimed joyfully. "I have four kids and an ex-wife, and she is still my best friend today, and Alex came into the family, and we all could not be happier. Alison is standing over there with our daughter." John pointed to her.

"And your wife was okay with you destroying your marriage because you wanted to be gay?" Barbara said in a hostile tone.

I stood quietly watching Mark's face as she continued to talk. I didn't come to John's defense because I knew he could take care of himself. Mark's head kept sinking lower and lower as if he were a whipped puppy as Barbara continued talking. John interrupted her.

"Staying in the marriage would have hurt her more. We worked hard to make things as easy as possible for the kids, and she forgave me, and we moved on," John stated firmly, looking directly into Barbara's eyes.

I felt so proud of John in that moment.

"If my husband had done that to me, I would have destroyed him. I would have taken everything I could and made it as hard as possible for him to see his kids," Barbara replied angrily.

"Well, I guess I was fortunate that I did not have a wife like you," John replied with just as much anger aimed back at her.

Barbara didn't like John's comment, but she didn't respond. Mark smiled slightly. Mark wasn't brave enough to stand up to her, but he enjoyed it when others did. As I listened to her speak, I knew that Mark's disappearance from my life was a blessing in disguise. If John had been anything like me, he would have walked away from that horrible creature. However, out of respect for Mark, someone he worked with, John shifted his mood from angry to friendly and continued talking.

"Whoever that guy was, I still thank him today for deciding to stop seeing Alex," John said happily. "Alex is wonderful to me, my family, and my children. Correction, our children," John joyfully continued.

For that comment, I had to kiss John on his cheek. Mark got a shocked look on his face.

"We have a great family, grandchildren, and friends, and our family keeps on growing," John added.

My tears wanted to flow, but I held them back. I felt so sorry for Mark, knowing that he was still living in a world of hell. John helped me find my courage, so maybe someone someday will help Mark find his.

Bobby can read me like a book, even from a hundred yards

away. He was standing with his mom and Dave, a little distance from us. He noticed I was getting emotional, I suppose, from my body language. He came over, hugged me, and took my hand.

"This is our youngest son, Bobby. He's eleven years old. He wants to play professional baseball someday," John stated as a proud father.

"What position do you play?" Mark asked Bobby.

"Second base, sir. I'm terrific," Bobby replied with confidence. John and I chuckled.

Bobby grabbed my hand, pulling me, and said, "Let's go, Pop. Let's go talk to Mom."

Before I walked away, I gave John another kiss on his cheek. I didn't acknowledge Mark or Barbara before leaving. It might have been rude to walk away without saying anything, but I couldn't think of any words to say.

I stood facing Alison and Dave as they continued talking with other parents. I had John in my sights the entire time. I watched as Mark and his wife walked away, leaving John alone for a moment, until another neighbor approached him. As Mark walked away, I saw him turn around to look at me with a sad expression on his face, or maybe it was a look of 'I'm sorry I hurt.'

John turned around and saw me standing in the distance, looking back at him. He gave me the look of 'Why are you not standing next to me?'

I said, "Excuse me," to Alison before Bobby and I walked over to John, with him still holding my hand.

"Why were Mark and his wife at this school when they live an hour away?" I asked.

"They moved closer to work about two years ago. The drive

was becoming too much for him. But how did you know that they once lived farther away?" John asked.

"I'll tell you later after we get home," I said. John kissed me softly on my lips.

"Let's get our tushes moving to Alison and Dave's house, everyone. The caterers should be cooking by now," John said loud enough for everyone in our group to hear.

"I am so hungry," Bobby cheered.

"Of course you are, sweetheart," Alison said as she patted Bobby on his head.

Alison handled all the arrangements for Sarah's graduation party. A gathering for a young lady was something John had no experience with, except for writing a check. Invitations had been sent out weeks earlier. Sarah's party was hosted at Alison and Dave's because their backyard was bigger than ours, mainly because they didn't have a pool. The caterers and their staff took care of everything so that our family could enjoy ourselves. However, keeping tabs on all the small kids running through the house and the teenagers sneaking off to a dark corner for a make-out session was exhausting.

The weather stayed perfect all day. Sarah requested a picnic-style menu for her party, featuring burgers, hot dogs, corn on the cob, baked beans, potato salad, desserts, and root beer floats. The grills were set off to one side of the backyard, the smoky grease rising into the air from the sizzling burgers.

After eating way too much, we all decided it was time for presents—-a good moment to let the food settle in our stomachs. As Sarah opened a present or an envelope with money, the crowd let out oohs and aahs. Fifty people were initially invited, but the number eventually grew to at least a hundred. Kids stopping by for a free meal, I guess. But it didn't matter,

Sarah was happy.

As the house emptied, Alison asked Bobby to stay overnight so he could spend more time with his grandparents. Alison's parents retired and moved to Palm Springs about five years ago, and they drove up for the occasion. Bobby loves visiting his grandparents because they like to spoil him.

John and I arrived home exhausted. He didn't say a word about Mark until we stepped through our front door.

"What was going on today? I didn't want to ask in front of anyone, but I was worried about you."

"I'm sort of afraid to tell you because you know Mark, and you work with him," I said anxiously.

" But what does this have to do with Mark that upset you today?" John asked caringly.

It still hadn't clicked in John's mind that Mark was my Mark from years ago. I could trust John with anything, so if I told him, I didn't think he would ever get mad someday and blurt it out or tell anyone; it would be a secret between us. I shared many secrets with John over the years, and I know he never revealed them to anyone.

"Remember the man who dumped me before I met you. And that he was coming out and that he wasn't divorced yet, and he had children. Well, it was ..."

John got a shocked look on his face and blurted out, "Oh my god, it was Mark."

John's mouth was moving, but no words were coming out, and then he continued.

"Everyone at work knew that Mark was in a bad relationship, but nobody ever thought that he was trying to come out of the closet," John said loudly and excitedly.

"Mark told me that he had never been attracted to a man

before, that he and his wife had many gay friends over the years and he'd never thought of having sex with any of them," I said breathlessly and nervously. John sat in silence while I spoke.

"He said I treated him so kindly the night we met. After his wife mistreated him on his birthday in front of strangers and friends, he just wanted to escape for a while and came dancing with me. After we got stoned, he needed some attention from someone, and he wanted it from me," I rambled, as John held my face with both hands.

"I got emotional today, not because of leftover feelings for him, but because he looked so sad. He's much heavier now and appears much older than he should. I felt bad for him, especially when Barbara started talking. I was so relieved she didn't remember me from the restaurant four years ago." I took a nervous breath. "I can't believe you work with Mark."

"It's a big company. I see Mark every day, but we are not friends outside of work. And I couldn't believe the things Barbara was saying about what she would do if he ever asked for a divorce. Mark must feel like a prisoner in his own home," John uttered with sadness in his eyes.

"Do you think Barbara suspects that Mark is gay, or maybe bi, and that is why she is so angry and has been for years?" I asked.

"Maybe?" John replied.

"Did Alison ever say she suspected that you were?" I asked.

"I never asked her, and she never said she did. But maybe I should ask her? We have talked about many things over the years, but I never asked her that direct question before," John said calmly.

John pulled me close for a hug and a kiss.

"Mark looked so sad today, and I was shocked to see him standing in front of me. I thought he lived farther away, which is why I got emotional. It all came crashing down on me. And leave it to Bobby to come save me," I said, smiling.

"I love that kid."

"He loves you, too," John said.

"So are you upset with me for anything?" I asked.

"Why would I be upset with you? I'm surprised to hear all of this, but you never really know what anyone is doing. But if you were the one and only man he's ever been with, he couldn't have found a better man to be his first," John said lovingly.

"Thank you for understanding, John."

"Understanding that we all have a past. I love you and I always will," John replied softly.

John paused in thought before speaking.

"What is it?" I asked.

"So, if Mark had continued to see you, you could have ended up in a horrible relationship with tons of problems because of his wife, and you would never have met me, and we would not be as happy as we are today with our family," John said sadly.

"No, we would not, and that is the saddest thought I have ever had. I love you and our family so much, John," I told him before kissing his lips gently.

"Me too," John said, returning the kiss.

"Do you know how proud of you I am right now?" John said caringly.

"Why?" I asked, puzzled.

"Because you have come so far in your life. A conversation like we just had about Mark would normally have thrown you into chaos, and you'd be bawling your eyes out and begging me not to leave you. Then you'd be asking me to fuck you so you could feel better. That's why I am so proud of you. You've become the man you've always wanted to be. You didn't do it for me, Bobby, or anyone else; you did it all for yourself. And you're finally able to admit that to yourself," John said so lovingly.

I had to cry a little because who wouldn't when hearing praise like that from someone who cared about you the way John cared about me. I thought of many things to say in response to his words, but I only said what I was feeling at that moment.

"Would you take me to bed and fuck me so I could make you feel better, my love?" I asked John seductively.

I wasn't feeling insecure; I just wanted to make love to my husband.

John chuckled and said, "Yes, please."

John took me by my hand and led me to our bedroom.

***

Morning came too soon. I wasn't ready to go back to work after an emotional and joyous weekend.

"Are you going to say anything to Mark about the weekend?" I asked John.

"Not unless he asks me a direct question about any of it?" John replied.

"What are you going to say if he does?" I said hesitantly.

"I will tell him the same thing I told you. We all have a past, and it has nothing to do with the present, and I would never say anything to anyone about it. So, let us all move forward," John said caringly.

"What if he asks why I was emotional when Bobby came to save me?" I said softly.

"I will tell him that it was out of your concern for him. You want the best for him. And now let's all move forward," John added.

"You are a wise man, John. I am so glad I have you," I proclaimed.

"Me too," John said as he kissed me goodbye before leaving for work.

16

Chapter Sixteen

"On your next birthday, you will turn fifty-five, and soon after, I will be turning fifty. We will have two milestone birthdays to celebrate within thirty days," John exclaimed excitedly.

"Is there anything special you want for your fiftieth birthday? Like you said, it's a big one," I asked, as I pulled him in for a kiss.

"Why don't you ask Alison? I know she and the kids will want to make a big deal out of it," John added.

"I want to make a big deal out of it, also," I said.

"All I want is a dinner with you and the guys at the Claim Jumper Restaurant in Long Beach," John replied.

"I love their Chocolate Motherlode cake, and their meals are so big it takes three days to eat them." I chuckled.

"No, Bobby?" I added.

"No, just us guys," John uttered and then kissed me.

The one thing I love most about John—well, I love everything about him—is that he is always looking for ways to take care of me, make me happy, and ensure I feel loved. I found the one person out of millions who thought I was someone special. Plus, I had a group of friends who never made fun of me and a young boy who thought of me as his best friend, his buddy, and his pop. Whether they knew it or not, they made me want to be a better, stronger person, not someone who cried and embarrassed them.

"Marino's in Toluca Lake is still your favorite restaurant, right?" John asked, already knowing the answer.

"Yes, sir, you are correct," I replied lightly.

"Great, because we are taking the entire family and our closest friends out to dinner. Then we and the guys are all going dancing," John said as he kissed me on my cheek. I smiled.

"Doesn't the family want to go with us?" I asked, chuckling.

"Well, Sam and Lisa want to go home to their kids. Sarah has made plans with her college friends, Bobby is going home with my parents, and can you see Dave and Alison in a gay bar?" John added.

"Never happening. Dave is a good-looking guy, and with all those young men in their early twenties who are looking for sugar daddies, they'd be on him like flies to honey. But it would be funny to watch," I said. John laughed.

"Bobby is going to hate that he can't come dancing with us, and he loves dancing with you."

"Hey, he'd dance with you too if you liked ABBA," I replied.

"Is my son gay?" John asked curiously with a little worried sound in his voice.

"No, he's not gay. He talks about girls with me all the time. He even asked me when he would be old enough to have sex," I replied with a chuckle. John's eyes bugged out.

"What?" John said quickly. I laughed.

"I told him he has a lot to learn about girls first. The most important thing is how to treat and respect them. Then, when he is a mature adult, his dad will tell him when that is, so get ready for that conversation. He'll do as all boys do until that time comes—he will grab it tight with his right hand and stroke it," I said with a big grin. "Bobby giggled when I told him about stroking it." John giggled. "Like father, like son, I guess."

"Why doesn't he talk to me about these things?" John asked with a bit of sadness in his voice.

"For some reason, he said he isn't as embarrassed talking to me. I told him he needs to get over his embarrassment and talk to you more because these are things that every growing boy goes through on their way to being an adult and that his father has been through them all."

A grin came to John's face.

"When Bobby asked me about sex, I told him that I needed to ask you if that was okay before I shared all the details of what intercourse involved. Or did you want to tell him yourself?" I asked John with a crinkled-up face.

John grimaced at the thought of telling another son about sex.

"Could you tell Bobby about everything? I had a tough time talking to Sam years ago. But Sam was so open about it all, I think he embarrassed me more than I could have embarrassed him," John muttered.

"I'd be happy to," I said excitedly. "I never thought that I would have a chance to have this talk with anyone. And now I have a son that I can pass all my wisdom to." I smiled. John looked relieved and laughed at me.

I was thrilled to have this opportunity to talk with my son—

my son, not just John's son, but my own. Bobby considered me his dad. He has often said that he had the best two dads ever. I don't remember a time when I didn't have John, our family, and our friends in my life. It now seems like my past life was just a dream, and I had finally woken up from my nightmare. The remnants of those dreams still float around in my head, but they no longer control me like they used to.

"I dated women until I was thirty, so I know all about them—they're icky. Just kidding." I chuckled. "Technically speaking, I am probably bisexual, like you are bisexual," I stated matter-of-factly.

"Dude, you are one hundred percent gay. I don't care how many women you've been with," John exclaimed, chuckling.

"Ha, ha!" I laughed. I continued talking, as if John hadn't responded to me.

"I enjoyed being with a woman. I liked sex with a woman."

"Did you?" John asked. I paused, thinking for a moment.

"I think so," I answered nonchalantly. "I fell in love with a woman, but something always seemed to be missing."

"Like I said, totally gay. You were just going through the motions to appease others." John chuckled again. "What was that? What was missing?"

"A woman never fulfilled me with everything I needed from a spouse, being held, making love, even talking to a woman never fulfilled me completely." I released a deep breath.

"Like I said, gay, gay, gay," John added.

"I hate you, John," I said sarcastically.

"No, you don't, you love me," John replied.

"Yes, I do, I love you," I said tenderly. John gently kissed my lips. "And that is why you probably decided one day, after years with your wife, that you needed something else, and that something was what a man could fulfill for you."

John thought about it but didn't answer me right away, as if he were taking my words seriously.

"Nope, I'm one hundred percent gay. I was just going through the motions to make everyone happy. My parents wanted me to have a family, and I didn't want to disappoint them. So I buried my feelings until I no longer could." John let out a sigh. "I would never tell Alison because I do love her, and she was my best friend. But I wasn't in love with her. Plus, I love making love to you too much to be anything else, sweetheart." John chuckled as I wrapped my arms around him.

John pulled away from me so he could look into my eyes.

"Talking about fulfilling our agreement," John said.

"Were we?" I asked curiously.

"No, but I thought it was a good segue into something I needed to talk about." John giggled.

" Okay," I answered.

"We are lucky that you like being on the bottom, and I like being on top. But it is the last Saturday of the month, and you get your turn on top tonight," John said cautiously. I looked at John, puzzled.

"I like being inside you, but I have to admit, I prefer being on the bottom much more. And you do such a great job being on top." I giggled. We both smiled.

"Even though I want to be on the bottom, it still hurts after all this time. I'm so thankful we have a gay doctor; I feel comfortable talking to him about personal issues. I've asked him during yearly physicals if there's something wrong down there, but he said everything looked just fine and there's no reason it should hurt like it does," John said.

"But, you like my tongue," I asked curiously.

"Oh my god, yes, I love your tongue," John said excitedly. "You go crazy down there, and you drive me nuts. And while you are using your tongue, I feel like I want more inside me. Plus, I've had dreams about you inside me, and it feels great. My legs are wrapped around you, we're pulsating our bodies against each other, I am moaning, and so are you, as our lips are tight against each other."

I breathed heavily after John described our lovemaking with me on top.

"I want to make you moan like that," I told John as I swallowed hard. John smiled.

"Do you think it could be psychological, and it's not a manly thing to do because you pretended to be straight for so long?" I asked cautiously.

John looked at me patiently before speaking. He didn't take everything I said seriously, but he didn't dismiss it as nonsense either. My nonsensical words might sometimes have sounded like a little boy talking, but out of the mouths of babes come words of wisdom.

"Never thought of that before. It's something to think about, and at my next physical, I will talk to the doctor about it," John said.

I smiled widely and kissed John hard on the lips.

"Why don't you talk to Dr. Smith about it instead of waiting several months until your next physical? If it's a psychological issue, don't you think Dr. Smith is a better fit?" I asked.

"We haven't talked to her in quite a while. Do you think she'd want to help again?" John replied.

"Of course she would. She loves us. She helped us after we came back from Hawaii with Bobby and had trouble letting go of him after those two wonderful weeks. And she did say that if we ever needed her, we should give her a call. Why don't you call her tomorrow?" I said as I kissed him.

"You're a wise man, Alex," John added.

"Yes, I am," I replied.

"You're also a butt head sometimes, my love."

"Yes, I am." I chuckled.

John pulled me onto the bed, and we lay side by side talking.

"Why don't we try pot tonight and see if it helps. Maybe it will relax you more. We don't use it very often. So maybe?" I asked softly. John grimaced. "And if it's not working, you can roll me over and do me. I know you like pot when I use my tongue."

"Yes, I do," John said joyously. "I don't know what it is about your tongue, but when you are down there, it seems like my entire body is energized. I feel as if I could have an orgasm without touching myself. I think it is more intimate than fucking or sucking," John said passionately.

"Thank you, sweetheart," I said, with a caring tone. John pulled me in close and kissed me hard.

"I never suggested rimming when I first met someone new, but from the moment we met, I knew I wanted to be that close to you. You intrigued me as you looked around the bar, searching for someone. And when you asked if I wanted a fuck or a dance, I was hooked. My heart started beating out of my chest from the moment you turned and smiled at me, and that is why I had to convince you to go to breakfast with me the next morning. You were the man that my friends wanted me to find to become my husband."

John could see that my face was ready to explode in tears. My heart was beating out of my chest. I took a deep breath to stop any tears. He leaned in to kiss me, and as he did, he reached down the front of my pants and played with my dick. I chuckled. I smiled from ear to ear and kissed him back.

"Tonight, I am taking care of you. If my tongue relaxes you enough, maybe you'll feel like you want more inside you. But if you can't take the little guy, we can wait until you talk to Dr. Smith," I said, smiling.

"You're the best," John uttered.

"Why did you have to start calling my dick 'the little guy'? You know how self-conscious I am about my size," I asked John hesitantly.

"I have never said it in front of anyone else, and you know I never would, sweetheart. I love you too much, and I am not the size queen in this relationship." John giggled. I frowned. "He's the perfect size for me. I love your dick because it is attached to the wonderful man I love," John said caringly.

"Thank you for loving me the way you do," I added.

"No problem. You are so easy to love." John chuckled.

I kissed him before I spoke again.

"Do you have two orgasms in you today?" I asked softly.

He smiled and asked, "Why?"

"Well, it's only two in the afternoon, and all this talk about the little guy has made me horny. We know Bobby won't be surprising us because he is gone for the weekend with Alison and Dave. So if you attack my bottom now, I promise I will do an above-average job on yours later tonight with either my tongue or the little guy." I giggled.

"You promise an above-average job tonight?" John asked with a moan.

"Yes, dear, I do," I replied.

"Then why are you not taking your clothes off, or do you want me to pull your pants down and bend you over the sofa?"

John added.

"Oh my god, you have to be the sexiest man in the world. Sofa, please."

John unbuckled my pants, pulled down the zipper, and lowered them to my ankles. He turned me around so I was facing the back of the sofa and bent me over it. He slapped my ass and told me not to move. He walked quickly to the bedroom for the lube. On his way back, he said, "This is so much fun." I chuckled.

He dropped his pants to his ankles and stepped out of one of the legs so he had more unrestricted movement. He slapped his hard penis against my ass, put lube on his dick, and then my butt. He slides inside me in one steady forward motion. A gasp came out of me, and I was in heaven. I could feel John smile as he said, "I love being inside you."

***

It's my fifty-fifth birthday, and I hadn't been back to Marino's on my birthday for five years. Not that I was afraid to run into Mark, but maybe I was. However, now that I had run into him at graduation and knew that John worked with him, perhaps it wouldn't be as awkward to see him and Barbara again. But then Barbara would remember where she had met me before, and I would prefer to avoid that conversation at all costs. I didn't know if this was Mark's favorite birthday restaurant or if it had been their first time. But after the uproar Barbara caused that night, she was probably asked never to return.

"Why are you so nervous tonight?" John asked.

"I'm not nervous," I replied.

"Yes, you are. You're acting like the big bad monster will walk into the room at any moment," John said caringly.

"Well, maybe I am," I answered.

"Are you worried about Mark coming here for his birthday tonight?" John asked.

"Yes, yes, I am. Sorry, but yes, I am," I blurted out.

"Let's find a quiet place to talk." John took my hand and led me outside. "He's not coming here tonight. I wished him a happy birthday at work today when someone brought him a cake, and I asked him what he had planned for the evening. He told me he was doing nothing tonight, but this coming Saturday, his kids are taking him to Disneyland to see all the Christmas lights, which they all loved. And he told me to wish you a happy birthday."

I released a heavy breath.

My eyes were filling with tears, but I chose to chuckle instead. Laughter had become my new way of coping, not sex, and a lot less crying. Sex was something I shared with John, where we had fun, laughed, and got silly together.

"You didn't mention Barbara. Isn't she going with them?" I wondered.

"No. Since graduation, and now that his kids are older, he finally told her he wasn't going to put up with her crap anymore." My mouth hung open, but no words came out. "And no, he didn't come out. He's still afraid, and he may never come out. But he's happier now that he stood up to her. They are living in the same house but leading separate lives."

"Wow, I'm so happy for him. At least it's a start for him to be happy. You two talk a lot, do you?" I asked curiously.

"We talked on Monday after graduation and again today. He doesn't have anyone to talk to and asked if I would listen. He knew you told me everything about the two of you, so it was easier for him to open up to me. But he didn't mention your relationship. He discussed what was happening in his life at home." John paused. "I'm not going to lose you to Mark, am I?" John asked softly.

I grabbed John's face with both hands and kissed him hard.

"Does that answer your question, your stupid question?" I said gruffly.

"Okay, I just wanted to make sure." John giggled.

"I love Disneyland at Christmas. Why don't we ask everyone if they want to go next week before all the lights are gone, and make a night of it?" I asked.

"Sounds good to me," John replied excitedly.

"We'd better get back to the party. It's my birthday. I am surprised that Bobby isn't hunting for us," I said. John grabbed my hand and guided me back to the banquet room, where everyone cheered as we entered.

Fifty-five was a milestone birthday, and ever since being with John, he had always made my birthdays special. I wished the numbers weren't getting so high. I had people from my past ask if they could join us for the celebration—people who once were too busy because it was the Christmas season and they had parties to attend. I believed that, over time, thanks to John, my insecurities had diminished significantly, and people could now tolerate me for longer periods of time. John said it was because of all my hard work that I am the man I am today. I got tired of debating the issue with him and agreed. I love that man, and I love myself.

"Dinner is just for family, but join us at Oil Can Harry's around ten p.m.," I'd told them.

I'd mentioned not to bring presents, but they knew how much I liked watches, especially unique or antique watches from the early 1900s. They all chipped in to buy a watch that John found in an antique shop during our last trip to New York City with the guys. Bobby was upset with us because he wanted to go, but it was for grown-ups only. He knew we traveled a lot with our friends, but we promised we would take him someday, and we never break our promises to Bobby.

I feel like the more self-confident I became, the more opportunities came my way. I found a new job where my boss didn't threaten to fire me every five minutes. One of my clients, who saw how hard I worked and how poorly my boss treated me, offered me a position at his production company. Over time, I received two promotions and two substantial raises. I loved that my new boss continued doing business at the same company I used to work at because now I was the client, and my old boss had to bow down and kiss my ass to keep me happy. My new boss gave me permission to get some revenge, but not to go overboard.

I enjoyed being a client at my old company because I made many friends there. I anticipated and resolved most foreseeable problems, which saved my new boss a significant amount of money, and he appreciated it. My old boss did not. I never socialized with coworkers outside the workplace at my old company. I kept work life and home life separate. They didn't know the insecure person my friends knew; they knew the hard-working professional my clients saw and appreciated. But they could tell there was a difference in me. Before, I was professional and pleasant; now, I am confident and happy. However, at my new company, I have made many new friends whom I see outside of the office.

***

John isn't the kind of person who needs a lot of fanfare to know he's loved. He enjoys caring for his family and me. He says that's all he will ever need. But for his fiftieth birthday, I wanted to make at least a good effort to show him how much I care. I sent him flowers and a large red velvet cake with cream cheese frosting—his favorite—to his office, along with fifty black balloons with the number 50 on them. Luckily, his office has a large courtyard where the balloons were taken and released into the air, and many co-workers cheered.

I received a phone call from John when he was fifteen minutes from home.

"Honey, get ready, because I'm going to thank you for my surprise today as soon as I walk through the front door," John stated.

"Yes, sir. I'll be ready," I replied.

It's not the first time I'd received a phone call like that. And ten minutes later, I was naked on the bed waiting for him.

"Thank you for my surprise today, sweetheart," John said softly as his blue eyes stared at me.

John placed his finger over his lips to tell me to keep silent as he stood next to the bed, taking off his clothes. I smiled as his hard dick sprang from his pants. He crawled between my legs, placing them over his shoulders, reached to the nightstand for the lube, and lathered up his dick and my butt. He slid slowly inside me till his body was against mine. His lips attacked mine, and we stayed like that until we both had our orgasms. An hour later, the guys knocked on our front door, yelling "Happy birthday!" when the limo taking us to the Claim Jumper Restaurant arrived.

***

One hundred people gathered at Alison and Dave's house two days later to celebrate John's birthday: family, friends, close neighbors, and a few out-of-town guests were invited. All the adult kids and Bobby stayed at Alison's for the weekend to help with the party. The guys stayed at our house so they wouldn't have to drive home afterward. Not that any of us drank a lot, but it was better to be cautious. Plus, it was always fun when the guys stayed over. Alison told everyone invited to John's fiftieth that there would be presents. John requested a higher-end menu than the last event, along with a band that played country western music.

An hour after the party began, John said, "Can we go home? I can't smile anymore after all these congratulations on getting old."

"You're not getting old, you're ripening well." I chuckled.

"Well, I want to ripen naked with you at home," John replied.

"We can't. We have a house full of company," I responded. John frowned.

"Let's go dance. You wanted a band, and they play country western. So go tell them to play three different line dances, and we'll get the guys and Bobby on the dance floor with us. You wore your cowboy boots tonight so you could dance," I added. "And when we get home, I want you in your boots and hat and nothing else. You can ride me till the cows come home, cowboy."

John's face lit up as if it were Christmas morning.

Everyone cleared the dance floor because no one knew how to dance to country western music. So, John, Bobby, the guys, and I formed two lines and started line dancing as the band played. Hoots and hollers filled the air as we danced. A few people tried their best to follow us, but some lost interest quickly. This was the distraction John needed to start having more fun at his own party. After our third dance, and before we left the dance floor, Bobby wanted to say something to his dad. He asked the band if he could use the microphone.

"I just want to wish my dad a happy birthday. He is the best dad ever. He takes great care of us all."

The crowd said, "Aww." in unison.

"And please stop telling him how old he is today. He knows it already," Bobby added.

"Bobby!" Alison blurted out in shock.

The crowd was silent.

"That's my boy." John laughed loudly.

The crowd broke out in laughter.

John, John, John, my all, my love, my everything. He loves me, and I never doubt it, and so does Bobby. I hope I've become a man they can both be proud of. I can feel the difference in me that they helped me achieve. I don't feel defensive around others like I used to. If anyone teases me, and I don't like it, I speak up. I don't cry like I did either. It was exhausting. But there are still appropriate times to cry, and I do.

17

Chapter Seventeen

Bobby had been living with John and me full-time since shortly after Alison and Dave got married, not because his mother doesn't love him, but because Alison and Dave were taking trips they wanted to go on alone. So it made sense for Bobby to live with us full-time, and we couldn't have been happier.

Dave was a great guy, but since this was his first and hopefully only marriage, he wanted to enjoy being a newlywed and getting to know Alison without the added responsibility of children to care for. We knew Dave loved Bobby and the other kids, but he still didn't want to be tied down by them.

"Bobby needs a full-time father in his life to provide the guidance a growing boy requires," Alison explained caringly.

Bobby would graduate from eighth grade in two weeks. He was one of the top players on the junior high baseball team and popular with his classmates, especially the girls. The girls kept pestering him to go on a date, but both John and Alison decided that junior high was too young to start dating and he should wait until high school.

Bobby was excited to become a teenager and start high school next September. He was becoming more independent and no longer needed us as much as he had. I was sitting on the back patio in my lounge chair, gazing into the sky, when Bobby came running into the house. That boy had so much energy. I was watching the planes that flew over our house, taking off from the nearby Burbank Airport. John was in the kitchen, preparing dinner. Bobby sat on my chair in front of me, so I pulled him into me for a good hug. John looked at us both through the kitchen window and smiled.

"You're getting so big," I told him as I squeezed him tighter. Even though he was becoming more independent, he was still my little buddy.

He was much smaller than most of the boys in his grade. However, he had a lot of strength in his smaller frame, which enabled him to hit all those home runs that helped his team secure second place that year. So he still fit perfectly in my lap.

"Do you want me to move and get my own chair, Pop?" he asked.

"Don't you dare. I hope you never get too big to sit with me."

"I won't, Pop, I promise."

Instead of getting emotional, John saw a broad smile on my face. I could see the lightness in John's expression now when he looks at me, replacing the worry I used to see in his eyes. Looking to the future, not the past, was my new goal.

John walked onto the patio through the French doors and said, "Dinner will be ready in about sixty minutes. I just put it in the oven."

"What is it?" Bobby asked with his face all crinkled up as if his dad were cooking something he didn't like.

"I hope it's not your healthy cooking," Bobby added.

John laughed.

"Healthy cooking is good for you. It helps you grow big and strong."

"I know," Bobby said sheepishly.

"Yes, tonight is, well, you're probably not going to like it much," John teased Bobby.

Bobby looked at his dad with a frown.

"Well, it's meatloaf with lots of cheese and sausage inside it, double-baked potatoes, and mac and cheese," John added, chuckling at Bobby.

"Oh my god ... I love you, Dad. That's my favorite."

Bobby stood up to give his dad a hug and a kiss. Then he turned around and said, "Pop, I'm sorry, I forgot to tell you hello when I came in and sat on you." He leaned down to give me a hug and a kiss.

"Don't ever get too big to hug and kiss us," I said.

"I won't, Pop. I love you both too much. Besides, that's what we do in this family, and it still drives Dave nuts." Bobby chuckled. John and I laughed.

"But I have to say, Dave kisses Mom almost as much as you and Dad kiss. I hope I get to kiss someone that much someday," exclaimed Bobby.

John leaned down and whispered in my ear, "I hope you had that talk with him by now."

I smiled at John and responded with a chuckle, "Yes, Dad, we had that talk."

"Why are you two whispering to each other?" Bobby asked.

"After your kissing comment, Dad wanted to know if we had the sex talk yet, and I told him we did." Bobby turned red. We all laughed.

"Okay, young man, please sit down, we have something to talk to you about before we eat dinner," John said more firmly than he meant to. Bobby had a worried look on his face.

"What did I do wrong now?" Bobby asked gruffly.

"Well, young man ...," John said.

I started laughing. Bobby smiled.

"Don't tease me like that. I was worried."

"Why would you worry if you didn't do anything wrong?" John asked, laughing.

"I don't know. Even when I think I am not doing something wrong, I might be doing something wrong."

Bobby sat back down in the lounge chair with me again, but Dad asked him to sit in another chair so we could both see his face. He sat down but looked worried again.

"Graduation is in two weeks, and we are having a party at Mom's house for you with friends and relatives, but Pop and I want to do something special for you. What do you want for a graduation present?" John asked.

An enormous smile spread across his face, and he yelled, "I want to go to New York City. I want to see the Statue of Liberty and go to a Broadway play, and I want to ...,"

"Hold on, son, all that costs a lot of money and takes a lot of planning."

"Please, Dad, Pop. You said you would take me someday, you promised."

I glanced at John, and he looked back at me. We both smiled.

"Well, if we promised, and we have never broken a promise to you yet, so yes, we can go," John replied joyfully.

"You are the best dads ever. When can we go?" Bobby asked.

"Well, it just so happens that Pop and I have already made

reservations to go to New York City the week after you graduate."

"You are the greatest!" Bobby sang out, then sprang out of his chair, hugged his dad, then came to hug me. But he moved so fast that he slipped past me and fell into the pool. I quickly got up to see if he was okay. By the time I checked on him, he was jumping around, splashing, and yelling, "We're going to New York, we're going to New York."

A voice called out from the house next door. "Congrats, Bobby." It was our neighbor Alister, who already knew we were taking Bobby to New York. He kept an eye on our house whenever we traveled, and we did the same for him. Bobby shouted back, "Thank you, Alister." Bobby splashed water at me.

"Pop, jump in?" Bobby roared.

Luckily I was already wearing shorts, so I kicked off my shoes and jumped right in.

"Dad, get in here!" Bobby said excitedly.

John kicked off his shoes and jumped in. We splashed each other and yelled, "We're going to New York!"

John heard the oven timer go off, so he got out of the pool to check on dinner. We hate burnt food. After searching the cabinet for towels and finding none, he stood at the French doors leading into the kitchen and took off his dripping-wet clothes, down to his underwear. He didn't want to track water through the house to grab some towels for us to dry off. Usually, extra towels are stored in the cabinet near the pool, but since Bobby is currently in the forgetful stage of growing up, he forgot to fill the cabinet that morning, as John had asked.

Bobby said with a smirk on his face, "I am so glad there are no girls in our house."

"Why?" John asked as he turned to look at Bobby.

"Because sometimes, I just want to run around in my underwear, and with girls around, you just can't." We all laughed.

John told us not to come into the house to track water; he would bring us towels. He got the towels and placed them on a chair outside the kitchen doors near the pool. He told us to dry off and put on some dry clothes for dinner.

"Pop, let's eat on the patio tonight, please," Bobby requested.

"That's a good idea," I replied.

John went to the bedroom to get some dry clothes and then returned to the kitchen to take dinner out of the oven.

"Would the two of you set the table after you dry off?" John asked.

Bobby and I dried off and then went to our rooms to change into dry clothes. When I got back to the kitchen, I grabbed plates, glasses, and silverware for the table.

Before Bobby returned from his bedroom, I told John, "You look hot in wet underwear." He chuckled. I leaned into John while holding the tableware and kissed him.

Bobby came around the corner into the kitchen and said, "Are you being romantic?"

"Yes, son, we are being romantic," John replied.

***

A week after Bobby's graduation, he was telling everyone that he was now a freshman in high school. He was so proud of himself, and so was the entire family. As soon as Bobby graduated, Dave and Alison were off on another trip. Alison called all her children daily to check in with them when traveling. However, because Bobby was much younger than the other children, she always wanted to make sure he was doing fine with her gone. Bobby never meant to sound ungrateful, but as long as he had his two dads, he never felt abandoned when his mom traveled. But when she was at home, he spent time with her almost every day.

Bobby was becoming a typical teenager; he was more independent and no longer needed the attention he'd had just a few years ago unless he chose to seek it. However, he was still very attached to his dad and me, and I was grateful for that.

When he traveled with John and me, not much had changed. He still liked being in the middle of us. Maybe things would change after he started high school, but on our trip to New York City, he was the same old Bobby. In the first-class section of the plane, he sat in the middle seat. It was a pretty long trip from Los Angeles, and Bobby could sometimes get anxious, so we made sure to bring plenty of activities to keep him busy. We brought several movies on the laptop that the three of us enjoyed watching together.

Before we left Los Angeles, we had to ask Bobby one thing, so we had to act like grown-ups for just a moment.

"We need you to stay close to us at all times and not wander off while in New York. It's a fun place to be, with many things to do, but it can also be dangerous for a young man to go off by himself," John explained to Bobby.

"I'm old enough to understand what you're telling me, Dad. But just in case I forget, would you please remind me?" he replied.

We both laughed and gave him a big hug. Bobby was at the age where things would go in one ear and out the other as quickly as we said them. So we knew he was going to forget.

At the airport, we got into a taxi just outside the baggage claim area to reach our hotel.

"Where to, gentlemen?" asked the driver.

"Tempo by Hilton," John replied.

Bobby was bouncing from window to window to see all the sights.

"I'm going to be a freshman in high school in September, and this trip is my graduation present from eighth grade," Bobby said excitedly to the driver.

"Congratulations! You're a lucky young man to be given a trip like this as a present," replied the driver.

"Oh, this is my dad and this is my pop. They are the best dads ever," Bobby said excitedly.

"I think they're lucky to have an appreciative son like you," the driver added.

"Yes, they are," Bobby replied.

The driver chuckled, and so did we as we hugged Bobby from both sides.

Our hotel was in Times Square, so we could walk or quickly grab a cab to get to our planned event. It was late afternoon when we arrived, so we sent our bags to our rooms and asked the front desk for the nearest Jewish deli. We had taken Bobby to a Jewish deli in Los Angeles before, but nothing beats a New York Jewish deli. No offense, Los Angeles.

"Have you been to New York before, gentlemen?" asked the lady at the front desk.

"My husband and I have, but not our son," I replied.

"Then you have to take him to Katz's Delicatessen for his first. Have you been there, gentlemen? It's an icon of New York," she stated.

"Yes, we've been there," John added.

"Grab a cab in front of the hotel. It's a quick cab ride. You won't regret going the extra mile, gents," she said in a casual tone.

***

Katz's was loud and crowded, and the lady who greeted us was louder than the noise from all the people talking and the sounds coming from the kitchen.

"Hello," she stated in a gruff voice.

She pinched Bobby's cheek, smiled at him, and said, "Hello, young man."

"Hello," Bobby replied, looking a little scared of her. John placed his arm over Bobby's shoulder and pulled him into his side.

"Let's get you all to a table. You look hungry," she said enthusiastically.

Bobby sat on one side of the table with John, and I sat on the other. Bobby watched the servers carrying large trays of food, weaving around each other like performers in an intricate dance. Every time a server passed our table with a tray full of sandwiches, Bobby's eyes would widen. He had never seen a sandwich so huge before. That's why I prefer a New York deli over others—the sandwiches and kosher pickles are enormous.

When our order arrived, our eyes widened again at the size of our sandwiches. We also ordered a bowl of matzo ball soup, featuring a large matzo ball in the center, which we were going to share. We grinned from ear to ear like three little boys.

John had ordered a pastrami on rye, Bobby got corned beef on rye, and I had chopped liver and turkey on wheat with coleslaw on the sandwich—not on the side. I first had this sandwich the last time we were in New York with our friends, and now I eat one once a month and make it at home. My homemade version isn't as good as the deli's, but it's a close second. I also ordered a side of cheese blintzes with strawberry preserves for us to share as dessert. John and I laughed as Bobby tried to bite into his sandwich. He couldn't fit his mouth around it. I snapped a photo to text to Alison.

After returning to the hotel, we told Bobby we needed to take a nap before our first Broadway show that night so we wouldn't be yawning or dozing off. Then, after the show, we'd go out for a late dinner just like a New Yorker. Bobby was excited about this because he wanted to see New York at night.

Before Bobby went into his adjoining room to take a nap, he said, "Dad, Pop, you forgot to remind me to stay close to you at all times. I might be all grown up now, but I still need you to take care of me and keep me safe."

"Sorry, son. We'll do better," John said.

John laughed, and I did too. We both hugged and kissed Bobby, then sent him to his room.

"Make sure your door is locked to the hallway before you take your nap," I said.

"Sure thing, Pop," he replied.

As soon as I shut the door between our rooms, John looked at me and ordered me to get my ass in that bathroom. I loved it when he was bossy.

"Just to be on the safe side, let me spend a couple of minutes alone in the bathroom first, please," I added.

When he entered the bathroom, my pants were gone, and so were his. He was hard, but I was not. John placed a towel on the floor and put me on all four, lubed me up, and entered me. I love a man who knows the difference between making love and pure sex. Today was going to be all sex, and I loved how he opened me up with no warm-up. I got hard quickly. I leaned down on my elbows, and he took me as hard as he wanted to. I was in heaven, and my heart was beating fast.

By the time he came, slamming hard against me, I was not

even close. I was enjoying him inside me too much. I loved the feeling of him moving in and out of me without playing with myself, and I'd forget to come. John could sometimes make me come that way before he did, and when he did, my butt muscles would tighten around his penis so that he couldn't pull himself out of me. But this time I didn't reach my orgasm.

He laid me flat on my back on the towel he had thoughtfully placed on the cold tile floor and took me into his mouth. He knew how to make me climax quickly by sucking hard at the head. I was about to come when he suddenly stopped. I felt worried that something was wrong.

"Nothing's wrong," he reassured me. "I'm hard again; can I fuck you?"

"Yes, please."

He put me on all fours again and entered me with the same force he was using just minutes ago. This man knew how to take care of me and what I liked. When it was just sex, like it was when he had me bent over something or for a quickie in the bathroom, I liked it hard. As he moved in and out of me, I muttered, "I love you, I love you, I love you," as I giggled in pure pleasure.

On my third "I love you," I reached my release. John could tell when I was having an orgasm because my butt muscles would tighten around him as he moved even faster inside me until his second release. I collapsed flat on the floor, stomach down, butt up. Still inside me, he fell on top of me as my butt muscles twitched. He said softly and lovingly with his lips against my ear, "I love you, too."

We climbed into bed to take our nap, our bodies tightly wrapped around each other as we gently kissed. I asked John, while lying in bed, naked—yes, naked. Bobby now knew to knock before entering.

"Where are we going to take Bobby after high school graduation?"

John laughed at me.

"Maybe he won't want to travel with us by then. Or maybe he'll think he's too old for his dads."

"Oh no," I stated firmly. "He will always want to travel with us, and someday it'll be him, his wife, and then him, his wife, and kids."

"We don't do that with the rest of the family," John replied.

"Yes, we do. We've all gone on family vacations before, with spouses and kids. But Bobby is different. He's our baby, and he always will be." I chuckled. "You're right, John. I will have a hard time letting go of him if that day comes. But that day will never come, I am sure of it," I stated as a matter of fact. John smiled and pulled me in for a kiss, and we fell asleep.

***

Our week in New York included three Broadway shows. Bobby was at a middle stage of life. Some plays were too mature for him, and others were too juvenile. It came down to drawing straws to decide which play to see. The final choices were *The Lion King, Wicked,* and *Chicago*. Bobby liked *Chicago* the most because of the music and the costumes the girls wore. He's growing up too fast.

We attended a concert at Madison Square Garden featuring James Taylor and Carole King. John and I loved it, but Bobby fell asleep. We went to the Today Plaza so Alison could see us on TV. There is a three-hour time difference between California and New York, so we took a selfie and sent it to Alison as a reminder to watch. We also went up a few very tall buildings; visited the site of 9/11, where we tried to help Bobby understand what happened and why; and saw the Statue of Liberty.

I told Bobby, "This was where my grandparents arrived from Italy in 1914." As soon as I said that, I knew it was a mistake, because John glared at me.

"Do you have parents, Pop? Or I mean, are they still alive? You never talk about them," Bobby asked. I grimaced.

I knew these were questions Bobby would ask as he grew older. And I knew I had to tell him the truth.

"That's a long story, and I promise I will tell you about them, but could we talk about them after we get back home?"

Bobby could always tell when I didn't want to talk about something. But I promised John that I was no longer going to let my past haunt me or control me. So if Bobby wanted to know more about my family, I would answer all his questions.

"No problem, Pop."

***

Bobby ate a lot of food. It seemed like every two hours, he was hungry. On our final day, Bobby asked, "Can we go to Katz's Delicatessen for lunch. I want to say goodbye to the lady we met."

"I thought she scared you?" John said.

"She was nice," Bobby replied. John pulled him in for a hug.

***

I woke up when I heard something like furniture moving in Bobby's room. I looked at the clock on the nightstand and was amazed that it was three a.m. I climbed into a pair of shorts and opened the door between our rooms. I saw Bobby sitting in a chair looking out the floor-to-ceiling windows onto Times Square.

"What are you doing up?" I asked. The chair was wide enough for me to sit next to Bobby.

"Isn't this amazing, Pop?" Bobby said in wonderment.

"What is?" I replied.

"Everything! It's three in the morning, and look at all the people down there—just as many as during the daytime. And look at all the signs flashing, and the colored lights. It's the best show I've seen all week, and it's free — we didn't pay anyone for it," Bobby said wide-eyed.

I didn't want to burst Bobby's bubble, so I didn't mention that our two hotel rooms cost several hundred dollars per night. Let him figure it out on his own when he has to pay the bill as an adult.

"What are you two doing?" John said softly from the doorway between the rooms.

"Watching the show," Bobby replied.

"Can I join the two of you?"

"Sure, come join us," Bobby said.

John pulled another armchair over and sat next to me. He kissed me on my cheek and reached past me and squeezed Bobby's shoulder. Bobby didn't say anything or attempt to move between us. Maybe he's coming out of his needing to be in the middle of us mode, I thought. Perhaps he is starting to grow up.

"Are you enjoying the show, Dad?" Bobby asked. "Isn't it amazing?"

"Yes, it is, son, it's amazing," John replied.

***

A few days after we returned home from New York, Bobby asked me more about my parents. I called John into the family room to sit with us as I told Bobby everything about them. I explained how mean they were to each other, and to my sister and me. They were unhappy people who wanted those around them to feel just as miserable as they did. One day, I decided I had to keep them at a distance and didn't want them anywhere near our family. I shared a softer version of my life because he didn't need to hear about the abuse we endured, mostly from my mother. He said he understood why I didn't want them close to us.

"We're all the family you need, Pop," Bobby said caringly.

"Yes, you are, Bobby. Our family is all I need," I added.

"Pop, I am so proud of you, you know that?" Bobby acknowledged.

"Why?" I asked curiously.

"Talking about sad stuff always makes you cry, but lately, it doesn't. I'm glad," Bobby said.

I let out a big laugh, so I didn't start crying. This was definitely one of those moments that would have made me cry in the past. John sat quietly, listening to my adult conversations with Bobby, just as he had told me once he loved to do.

"I'm glad too, Bobby," I added.

John came over to the sofa, sat next to Bobby, and pulled us both in for a hug.

"I love you two so much," John said.

"I love you, too," Bobby and I said in unison.

***

John walked onto the patio from the kitchen, carrying a tray of steaks and raw veggies to cook on the grill, smiling.

"Why the big smile?" I asked.

"Remember this date, sweetheart. June 26th, 2015, when same-sex marriage became legal," John announced excitedly.

Bobby and his girlfriend, Emily, a two-year couple, both juniors in high school, rose from their chairs and cheered along with John and me.

"If you want to marry me, you're going to have to ask me. I am not asking you twice, my love," John added.

I froze in place as the three of them stared at me. Emily was like a third daughter. They met in their freshman year and are two peas in a pod. They talk every night, attend all school functions together, and join in many of our family gatherings.

"I'll be back in just a moment," I said.

Everyone had a puzzled look before I walked quickly into the house. I went to our bedroom, took a small box from the dresser, placed it in my pocket, and returned to the patio. I stood in front of everyone as calmly as I could. I had no fear of asking John this question. I knew he loved me.

"Remember when we went to Montreal last year with the guys?" I asked.

Bobby interrupted me, "I do. You didn't take me."

John and I laughed.

"Do you want us to take you to Montreal?" John asked.

"Yes, I do," Bobby replied.

"Well, I promise we will take you, and we have never broken a promise to you yet," John said, smiling.

Bobby grinned widely.

"Sorry, I still enjoy our trips," Bobby told John and me.

"Maybe we can take Emily with us if her parents will let her go," John said.

Emily's eyes widened.

"Can we, really, Dad?" Bobby roared.

"We'll talk to her parents and see?" John added.

"Anyway ... getting back to our trip. When we were in that jewelry shop you liked so much, where you bought yourself a new watch, we also looked at rings, just in case the marriage act passed," I said, grinning.

John looked at me, chuckling, knowing what I was about to say.

"Well, I bought those rings."

"Oh, Pop," Bobby uttered.

Emily, Bobby, and John were grinning from ear to ear.

"I wasn't planning to do this until the family and all the guys were together, but I figure I'd better do this now before I lose the element of surprise. And I wouldn't do this without Bobby here," I said.

I turned to Bobby to ask him to record this on his phone, but Emily was already standing behind him, recording us on her phone.

"Emily," I said. "You fit into this family just fine." I smiled at her. She returned my smile.

"So, I am getting down on one knee today to ask you the most important question I will ever ask, and I never thought in my lifetime I would be able to ask anyone this. So ... would you make me the happiest man on this planet and become my legal husband for the rest of our lives?"

John was chuckling with a few tears on his cheeks, and I hadn't cried, but I was ready too. John hadn't said a word, but I saw his lips quiver as he tried to speak.

I looked John straight in his eyes and said, "If you are going to say no just to tease me, I am going to throw you into the pool, I promise."

John laughed.

"Of course I will, you goof. Yes, I will marry you," he said passionately.

John reached out his hand to help me stand up. At nearly sixty years old, my joints needed a little help when rising from a kneeling position. As we hugged and kissed each other, Bobby joined us, and as usual, he got between us. He no longer has to stand on a chair to get his hugs and kisses, but he does have to stand on his toes just a little. We kissed each side of his face. Bobby reached his hand out to pull Emily in to share the hugs and kisses.

Emily's phone was still recording, propped up on the patio table, when she said, "Where are the rings?"

We looked at each other and laughed.

"They're in my pocket. I forgot about them," I said, embarrassed.

I pulled them out of my pocket, held them in front of John, and opened the case.

"Those aren't the ones I picked out," John uttered.

An 'oh my god' look appeared on my face until John said, "I'm just kidding, I love them."

I looked at John and said, "I hate you."

"No, you don't, you love me," John replied.

"Yes, I do, I love you," I said as we held each other tightly, with Bobby hugging Emily, who was standing off to our side. I believe this was the first time Bobby had ever let us go to hug someone else. I think the sex talk I'd had with him worked.

We took the appropriate rings and placed them on each other's fingers. As I kissed John, Bobby pushed us into the pool. As soon as we surfaced, we heard Bobby yelling with his hands waving in the air, "We're getting married," and he jumped into the pool. After splashing each other, Bobby told Emily to jump into the pool, and she did. We splashed each other for a few minutes before getting out of the pool to dry off.

"Well, who's going to get the towels?" John asked, staring at Bobby.

"Sorry, Dad. I forgot to fill the towel cabinet this morning."

Bobby grimaced.

Bobby told Emily to turn around until he gave her the okay to look. He stood at the French doors leading into the kitchen, took off all his clothes except his underwear, and said, "I'll get the towels."

We decided to have a small backyard ceremony with family and close friends, followed by a reception just thirty days after our engagement. Our yard was perfect for an evening gathering, with garden lights, pool lights, and candles flickering on the tables across the yard; it looked stunning. Bobby was my best man, and Sam was John's, just like before. Planning a wedding in thirty days took a lot of effort, but with our family's help, we made it happen.

During the ceremony, I kept thinking about how I had gotten here, how lucky I was to have found John. It wasn't just about how much John loved me, but also about how deserving I was of being loved. I liked myself now, and I truly loved myself. I loved the person I had become—something I never thought I would say or believe. John has been my rock, supporting me until I was able to stand on my own two feet. However, it was also something Bobby said at seven years old about his friend, whom the older boys picked on because he wouldn't defend himself. He couldn't fight the boys for his friend; he had to stand on his own, or he was going to be bullied for the rest of his life.

One last thing I forgot to mention: I took John's last name as my own.

18

Chapter Eighteen

Eight years after John and I were legally married, and sixteen years after I asked John if he wanted a fuck or a dance, Bobby, also known as Robert, professionally, and his wife, Emily, his one and only girlfriend whom he met in his first year of high school, gave birth to twins—one boy and one girl. The boy's name was Robert Allen Montgomery Jr., and their daughter's name was Emma Louise Montgomery.

I wish I had met John many years earlier, so we could have spent more time together. But if I had, it probably wouldn't have been the same life we have now. Timing is everything. Maybe I needed to go through that tough time with Mark so I would be ready to take a chance on a good man like John. Until John, I still believed all the nasty crap my parents told me: "You're worthless, you're no good, you're stupid, you're my worst mistake in life."

John tells me he fell in love with me the night we met, and I believe him. Though he may have treated me like a young child sometimes, that's because, in many ways, I was still a little kid even at fifty years old. Parts of me couldn't mature. I could crawl into his arms and cry; he would hold me tight until I was done, until all my pain escaped me. The pain that had seeped into my body over the fifty years before he met me.

John never made fun of me or told jokes at my expense, unlike Frank, the man who came to my fiftieth birthday dinner whom I had dated twenty years before. John gave me a loving home, a caring family, and six great friends. I don't hesitate to tell anyone I have four kids and several grandchildren. I love them all very much. I might love Bobby a little more than anyone else in the family, but that's because I've had him since he was young, and back then, we were both emotionally the same age—just two little boys who John watched playing together in the backyard.

I believe John was more brilliant than he realized. Maybe he gave me Bobby for a time at the beginning of our relationship because he knew that was the person I needed to help me heal. I didn't have much of a childhood because I was always searching for ways to protect myself from being bullied. However, on our trip to Hawaii when Bobby was young, John knew it was time to bring us back into the fold.

When the twins were three years old and Emily was pregnant again, still not showing, with their second set of twins — two boys this time — we took Bobby, Emily, and the three-year-olds to Hawaii for a week before the rest of the family joined us for a second week of vacation. Everyone in the family knew that we spoiled Bobby a little more than anyone else. However, no one seemed to mind, since the last child is often treated as the baby of the family.

Our first week in Hawaii was a delayed graduation gift for Bobby and Emily. We had planned to take them on vacation right after college, but first, they got married, then started new jobs, and Emily discovered she was expecting twins. Bobby hurt his left knee sliding into home plate during his freshman year of college, and it didn't heal properly. Because of that, he had no chance of playing professional baseball, as he had wanted, so he switched his major to finance. Bobby and Dave grew closer as Bobby moved into adulthood. After college, Bobby began working for Dave's Financial Consulting Firm as an investment advisor, and perhaps someday Bobby would take over Dave's firm, as Dave had no children of his own.

John and I were waiting for the day when Bobby wouldn't need us anymore, like the older kids did when they grew up and started their own families. But that day never came with Bobby; he still needs us, just as he always has. And when Emily came into his life and saw the closeness between the three of us, and jumped into the pool with us many years ago while they were in high school, she became our third daughter.

Spending a week with Bobby, Emily, and the kids was so much fun. I don't think we stopped laughing for the entire week. On the flight to Hawaii, we sat in the first-class section, which gave us more room to accommodate the twins. Bobby and Emily tried to keep the twins in their own seats, but they wanted to be near Grandpa and Gramps.

It had been a while since we traveled with small children, so we planned ahead with a few toys and plenty of their favorite movies on a laptop. I don't think Bobby and Emily minded the kids on our laps, because it gave them some alone time—much-needed alone time. They were cuddled up together, whispering in each other's ear and sneaking in a few kisses. John looked at them with a smile and said, "I guess the sex talk you had with Bobby years ago paid off." I laughed.

The twins looked at us with puzzled faces after Grandpa said the word sex.

"Language, please," I uttered. "Little ears." John smiled.

I distracted the twins with toys before they could ask, "What's sex, Grandpa?"

"No," I told John. "He had two excellent teachers. He just saw how loving we were to each other over the years."

I leaned over to kiss John. Little Bobby looked at us inquisitively and said, "Are you being romantic?"

John and I started laughing, and so did Bobby and Emily. The twins had heard their daddy say that to us many times.

Grandpa replied with a chuckle, "Yes, Bobby, we are being romantic."

Little Bobby and Emma loved singing with Grandpa and me at home. To entertain the twins and prevent their yelling from disturbing other passengers, Grandpa and I joined in, singing softly. A few minutes later, some other first-class passengers joined in and sang along with us. The twins sat in our laps, facing us. By the end of the song, everyone in first class was singing together.

Bobby pulled out his phone, recorded the sing-along, and sent it to Alison. We were very loud in the first-class section with our song after others joined in. Before our second song finished, people sitting in coach, with small children nearby, started singing along with us. After one last song, the twins got bored and wanted to watch a movie. When the song ended, the entire plane, full of people, clapped and cheered. Within minutes of watching their favorite movie, a story with dragons, the twins were sound asleep in our laps.

We stayed at our favorite hotel on Waikiki Beach. We had adjoining rooms so we could help take care of the twins. We told Bobby and Emily that when they wanted some time alone, they shouldn't be shy; we would take the kids for an outing.

"Don't forget, Gramps and I were young once, too," John uttered.

I hit John on his shoulder and said, "What do you mean used to be? We still are."

John whispered in my ear, "Yes, yes, we are, sir," and kissed me.

Bobby looked at us with a large smile and said, "I know I don't say it as much as I used to, but I love you two so much, and you are the best dads ever." Bobby gave us both a hug and a kiss. Then Emily joined in with a hug and a kiss for all three of us. The twins came running over, yelling in unison, "Pick me up, pick me up."

"Kisses, kisses," Emma shouted.

Everyone was kissing and hugging the twins.

"What a great family we have," I said cheerfully.

We all nodded in agreement.

We spent our first week doing everything we did the first time we took Bobby to Hawaii. Emily had never been before. She didn't travel much growing up because her parents didn't earn enough to spend on travel. However, she had wonderful parents; they gave her and her siblings all the love any child could want.

We began our first night in Hawaii playing pirates on the beach across from our hotel after enjoying a delicious dinner at the hotel's restaurant. Bobby told the twins the pirate story from his first trip with Grandpa and Gramps. Even though we had two girls with us this time, they were just as excited about playing pirates as the boys. We split into two groups: Emily, Emma, and Grandpa played the settlers, trying to recover their gold from the evil pirates who had stolen it. Emma always wanted Grandpa on her team, and Grandpa didn't argue. Bobby, little Bobby, and I were the pirates they tried to recover the treasure from. After a brief skirmish, the settlers emerged victorious. We played until the sun began to set. We sat huddled together on the beach and watched the beautiful colors in the sky fade away into the horizon.

We left the door open between the two rooms when we all went to bed. We were all exhausted and fell asleep within seconds.

When John and I woke in the morning, it was to two little voices, yelling at the top of their tiny little lungs, "Grandpa, Gramps, get up, I'm hungry."

I had déjà vu of Bobby saying the same thing when he was seven. They started jumping on the bed and didn't stop until we held them down and tickled them. They had the most wonderful little laughs, and we laughed along with them. We get lots of hugs and kisses from them after the tickle fest.

"I'll take care of the kids while you both get ready for the day," Bobby uttered.

Emily stood in the doorway, nodding in agreement.

"That is, unless you are going to get romantic in there and take a long time," Bobby chuckled.

John turned around quickly and looked at Bobby.

"What do you mean?" John said sharply.

Bobby laughed.

"I may not have known what you were doing the first time we came to Hawaii, but I figured it out the second time we were here, when I was older," Bobby said with a big grin, and so did

Emily, still standing at the door between the rooms. We all laughed.

Bobby closed the middle door as he took the kids back to their room. John grabbed my hand and pulled me into the bathroom, locking the door behind us.

"I hope we're not too old for this." John chuckled.

I smiled at him and responded, "I sure hope we are never too old for this."

We took our pants off at the same time, and we're both hard.

"Hey, they still work." I chuckled.

"And you are still as handsome as you ever were," John said caringly.

He lubed up my butt and both our penises and bent me over the sink.

"I love you so much," John uttered.

He kissed the back of my neck and entered me. I loved it when he filled up my backside.

John giggled and said, "Remember the conversations we used to have on vacation when Bobby was seven years old and I told you how much I needed you."

"Yes, I do."

And without losing his rhythm while moving in and out of me, he said, "I still need you that much, my love."

"I still need you that much, also," I replied.

We both had our releases, and into the shower we went, so we could get out quickly and help with the kids.

Everyone was excited about going ziplining.

"Pick who you want to be attached to for ziplining," Bobby told the twins.

Before they had a chance to decide, John and I told them that they should do this with their parents.

"This is something you should experience with Mommy and Daddy," Grandpa stated.

They smiled and said, "Okay, Grandpa. Emma very seldom disagreed with Grandpa.

"You won't be lonely, will you, Grandpa, Gramps?" Emma asked in her cute little voice.

"No, we'll be fine. Grandpa is going first so he can catch everyone. Then I am going last so I can make sure everyone made it safely," I told Emma. She smiled.

They were very much like their parents. They didn't get scared easily—two little daredevils soaring through the air, attached to Mom and Dad; laughter and squeals escaped from their tiny lungs. We've never lost Bobby; he still loves being close to us, and so do Emily and the kids.

On the night before the rest of the family arrived in Hawaii, we took a helicopter ride over Waikiki Beach, just as we had done when we met Oliver, right after his husband had died. I sat in the front seat so that Emily, Bobby, and Grandpa could sit in the back and hold the kids. We apologized to the pilot before boarding because of the not-so-quiet children we had with us.

The pilot laughed.

"Don't worry, folks, the headphones will block out most of the noise. I've had many young children on board before," the pilot said.

The next morning, the hotel sent two large vans to pick up the rest of our family and our friends from the airport. The hotel didn't usually get such large groups at one time. When the vans pulled up in front of the hotel and everyone exited, we all started hugging and kissing each other. We first greeted all the small kids, moving from child to child, and then we moved from adult to adult. It was a chaotic scene. The doorman and the parking attendants thought we were a surprise flash mob. It looked like a dance, but there was no music.

All our rooms were located on the same floor, allowing us to stay close to one another. Everyone gathered in our room to discuss the week's plan. Alison was always responsible for organizing us. With all the noise, I thought Dave's eyes were going to pop out of his head. He decided to go back to his room, and Alison would update him when she returned to scold him for leaving and then hug and kiss him.

We did most everything together, but sometimes we split into groups to do our own thing. Alison kept track of everyone through text messages—that's what moms do, and she's excellent at it.

One night, John, I, and the guys needed a break from the kids, so we went to a luau. Alison and Dave went off by themselves for a romantic evening and turned off their phones. By the time we got back to our room, Bobby, Emily, and the kids were all asleep. John quietly locked the center door and told me to get into the bathroom for a shower so he could kiss me from top to bottom, and he wanted the same from me after we got into bed. We had just gotten into bed when it was my turn to kiss John from head to toe, when I heard the twisting of the doorknob between the rooms. We froze, looking at each other.

"Did you hear something?" John asked.

A tiny knock on the door and then a soft voice. "Grandpa, I'm hungry," Emma said.

Then another soft knock, and another soft voice. "Gramps, me too," little Bobby added.

"Be right there," I said quietly, as the clock shone 12:01 a.m.

I opened the door, and two smiling faces looked up at me. I

looked into their room, and Bobby and Emily were sound asleep. The kids must have worn them out.

"Bobby?" I said softly.

I had to repeat myself a couple of times before he woke up. Emily also woke up as Bobby turned to look at me.

"What's wrong?" Bobby asked.

"Grandpa and I are taking the kids downstairs for something to eat," I said.

Bobby laughed.

"Give us one minute, and we'll go with you."

The twins cheered.

"Softly," Grandpa told the twins. They cheered again softly.

I must be the luckiest man in the world to have found a man like John. I know I've said this before, but I can't help myself. I could go on forever talking about him, but there are not enough words in the English language or any language to describe how I feel about this man and for the family he gave me—the children, grandchildren, in-laws, and ex-wife. Alison had become a great friend to me. Plus, Harry, Ben, Paul, Bob, Carlos, and Mike are the best friends anyone could ever want. We are all retired now. We travel a lot and have a great time together. We don't swim naked at the bottom of waterfalls anymore, because who wants to see an old man's sagging butt?

***

John and I called Bobby from our hotel in Italy, which feels more like a large villa in a small town just outside Tuscany. We had Bobby on speaker so we could talk to him at the same time. Bobby asked if we would take him, Emily, and the kids to Italy someday. We both laughed.

"Can't you afford your own trips by now?" John replied.

Bobby laughed, and so did Emily from the background.

"We like it when you pay for them. You know how much we love traveling with our dads." Bobby chuckled.

"Of course, we will, son, we promise. Have we ever broken a promise to you yet?" John said caringly.

"No, Dad, Pop, you never have," Bobby replied.

"Pop and I have never been to Rome. How about Rome?" John exclaimed.

We could hear Emily in the background yelling, "I like Rome." We laughed.

"Next year, then, we promise," John replied happily.

"Pop is falling asleep in my arms, so I'd better get us off to bed before I can't wake him up," John said softly.

"Where are you sitting?" Bobby asked.

"We are on the patio outside our room, watching the lights from the different villages. They are so beautiful," John said.

"Are you being romantic?" Bobby snickered.

"Yes, son, we are being romantic," John said softly.

"That's nice," Bobby mumbled. "Well, goodnight, Dad, Pop, I love you both so much."

"We love you too, son, Emily, and all the kids," John muttered tiredly.

"Goodnight," I yawned to them all.

"You are the best dads ever," Bobby said.

John and I looked at each other as he ended the call, and with a smile on our faces, we both said, "I love that kid."

The End

II

Thank You

Thank you so much for reading my debut novel. Your support and encouragement mean everything to me, and I genuinely appreciate every reader who has joined me on this journey. I hope my story has touched you in some way, and I look forward to sharing many more adventures with you in the future.

Brent Michaels

About the Author

Starting a career writing Gay Fiction novels at seventy-three might seem unusual to some, but for me, it's a way to share my life experiences and memories. It also helps me maintain my mental well-being. I can express all my thoughts, both good and bad, on paper.

Of course, there are moments of doubt, especially when exploring new technologies or adjusting to shifting publishing trends. Still, these challenges remind me that learning never truly stops, and creativity has no age limits. I appreciate the chance to start this journey, share my voice and stories, and show that it's never too late to follow a passion.

You can connect with me on:

https://www.facebook.com/Brent.Michaels.Author

www.ingramcontent.com/pod-product-compliance
Lightning Source LLC
LaVergne TN
LVHW010651110826
845149LV00014B/3037

* 9 7 9 8 9 9 4 4 1 4 2 0 0 *